Y0-CBT-420

NORTHERN LITES

A Brave New Wildwoods

By Don Oakland

Oak Press
904 Broadway Ave.
Wausau, WI

Copyright © 1990 by Don Oakland

All rights reserved. No part of this book may be reproduced or
transmitted in any form or by any means, electronic or mechanical,
including photocopying, recording, or by an information storage and
retrieval system, without permission in writing from the publisher.

ISBN 0-9615242-2-7

Published by:
Oak Press
904 Broadway Ave., Wausau, WI 54401

Distributed by:
Adventure Publications
P.O. 269
Cambridge, MN 55008

1-800-678-7006

Printed by
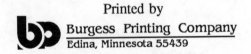 Burgess Printing Company
Edina, Minnesota 55439

DEDICATION

I dedicate Northern Lites to Jean Duncan, Brent Brye and Lucy Nitz, Lowell and Ruth Schleicher who read early drafts of my stories and suggested changes that significantly improved my stories (and found more spelling and grammatical errors than fleas on a dog's back); to my wife Kathy, whose constant and unswerving encouragement made this book possible; to my two daughters, Sarah and Melissa, who will probably kill me when they become old enough to read; to Cynthia Schley, whose creative talents, advice and support are no less than indispensable, and to the Canadian Canoe Crew: Lowell and Chris Schleicher, Bob and Rick Miller, Nick Bosley, Paul Phillips and Bill Krueger.

About the author and artist

Don Oakland lives in Wausau, Wisconsin where he is a writer/ editor at Wausau Hospital Center. A newspaper reporter for 14 years, Don wrote a popular outdoor column called The Wildwoods which inspired him to write two books, Wildwoods Weekly Reader and Wildwoods Dad, both in their second printing.

Cynthia Schley is a graphics artist living in Appleton, Wisconsin. She does freelance artwork and is currently working on her own humorous book.

TABLE OF CONTENTS

THE CANOE CREW CHRONICLES

Canada's Curse is the worst

I call it Canada's Curse.

It's a river in southern Ontario. It's not a spectacular river. It doesn't have thrilling rapids, gorgeous vistas or abundant fishing.

Instead it gives those who paddle up its waters backaches, swollen ankles, skinned shins, broken paddles and damaged canoes.

Every year we run from the comforts of home to the wilderness experience— five days of roughing it along this relatively nondescript river.

Every year we venture up the river and every year we wonder why we return.

I call the river Canada's Curse for two reasons. I can't pronounce the river's true name. It's a word so long you could make a sentence out of it. It's probably an Indian word for "Up Yours White Man."

The second reason it's a curse is that the river is deceptively peaceful. You think it will be an easy paddle. And it begins as an easy paddle. Then when you are beyond the point of reasonable return, it lowers the boom. It gets miserable. It gets arduous. And then it rains. And when the sun eventually comes out, so do the bugs.

A trip to the river begins easily enough. You have to cross a long lake ringed by picturesque bluffs of granite and pine. As you paddle along the shore, you think about how great it is to be outdoors and about the beauty of the lush growth of trees above outcroppings of wind etched granite.

After about an hour and a half, you come to the end of the lake and to the first portage. It is an easy portage. The trail is wide and free of brush and rock and fallen trees. It rises slowly and gently from the lakeshore, weaves through woods of pine and birch and then gradually winds down a hill to the next lake. A piece of cake, you think. Except you don't realize that on the other end of that portage is a dead lake. It was murdered one day by a local resident with a handful of dynamite. He didn't particularly like folks from the States fishing his lakes, so he blew up a beaver dam which was holding back most of the water in this small lake along the canoe route.

Soon the lake became a nightmare of muck, exposed logs and sharp, slippery rocks. Instead of being an easy 20 minute paddle, the lake had become a two-hour portage deterring all but the most masochistic canoeists.

When you finally reach the other side of the dead lake, you face a 45-minute portage up a steep hill and down a narrow trail crisscrossed with fallen trees and overhanging limbs. The trail ends with a steep slope which is always muddy. To get down it, you have to sit and slide down with your gear on your back. As you quickly descend the slope, rocks scrape up against your butt and legs.

Finally you reach the river. It has a gentle flow which is not difficult to paddle against. You think the worst is over. There are no rapids marked on the map. There are no more long portages, just a quiet meandering river slicing through the timberland and marsh.

You are tired, but you know the camp is just ahead. The paddling is relaxing, soothing to the muscles overstressed by the last portage and by the crossing of the dead lake. The sun is shining. The birds are singing. The wind is carrying the smells of the woods across the bow of your canoe.

Then the river springs its trap.

The sun quickly disappears behind gray clouds. A fine rain fills the air as you scramble to get your rain coat, which you put in the bottom of your pack because you didn't think you would need it right a way.

Suddenly the wind picks up with such force you feel like you are paddling up a wind tunnel.

But the camp is just around the next bend, you say to yourself.

Instead around the next bend is a logjam a hundred yards long, a mess of fallen timber that's impossible to traverse. And because logjams aren't permanent fixtures of the river, there aren't any portage trails around them.

So you get out of your canoe and sink into muck up to your thighs as you unload your gear. And you throw the packs on your back and crash through thick brush hoping to find a trail. Instead you find fallen branches which grab at your legs, and overhanging branches which rip at your raincoat and rocks covered with slippery moss which makes walking akin to crossing an ice rink on roller skates.

But the camp is just around the next bend, you tell yourself.

Instead around the next bend are rock shallows, where the river has lost its energy and the gravel it carries has been deposited onto rock bars over which only a few inches of water flow.

3

You get out, tie a rope to the bow and pull. Without paddlers, the canoe is light enough to just barely float over the rocks. However, every few feet the keel gets hung up on a large rock and you must pull with all your strength to free it. Meanwhile, the cold water circulates in your boots and chills your toes. It's like standing barefoot in a snowbank.

But the camp is just around the next bend, you assure yourself.

Instead there is a beaver dam four feet high. Everyone gets out of the canoes, and like pallbearers lifting a coffin they stand on either side of each gear-ladened canoe and carry it up and over the dam.

But the camp is just around the next bend, you tell yourself with each painful paddle stroke.

You soon realize that in the wilderness, every bend in the river looks the same. There are no signs. There are no distinguishing characteristics. Just a lot of trees and brush.

Hours pass and the sky grows dark.

You have portaged around five logjams. Your back aches from lifting full canoes over three beaver dams. Your feet are cold; your legs and ankles are sore from pulling the canoes across rock bars.

You have given up all hope of ever seeing camp. You begin to look for alternative campsites along the banks. But everywhere you look, the trees are too close, the ground is too rocky or the bank is too steep.

You have forgotten about that leisurely supper around the campfire. All that occupies your thoughts is getting that tent up, getting your boots off and crawling into the warmth of your sleeping bag, which, unbeknownst to you, lies soaking in a pool of river water in the bottom of your canoe.

Finally you reach camp.

You quickly set up your tent and change into dry clothes. If you are lucky, someone else in your party has finished before you and has started the campfire.

You pull your sleeping bag from the canoe and discover it resembles a dish sponge.

The cook announces supper is ready. Your spirits momentarily rise because all you have in your stomach are those three Snickers bars you munched on between portages.

You have visions of steak and fried potatoes. You get warmed over baked beans and soggy bread. "Guess the food can wasn't water tight," the cook apologizes.

At least the coffee is hot, you tell yourself.

At least the beans are filling, you mumble.

And, at least, tomorrow will be better.

Except it won't. That's Canada's Curse.

Canoe Crew challenges the outdoors

What breed of man would submit to such self abuse as Canada's Curse?

There are six of us who have taken the trip over the years. Others have joined us, but have never volunteered to go along a second time.

For most of us, the Canadian trip is our only venture into the wilderness. Wilderness being defined as outdoors without an outhouse.

Some of us are hunters. We'll go out for an afternoon and trudge through a woods in search of grouse or rabbit. A couple times, we'll venture out for a day in hopes of bagging a deer.

Some of us are fishermen. We'll go out on an afternoon and paddle along the banks of a nearby lake in hopes of hooking a small perch or bass.

Some of us are weekend campers. We'll take the family to

a state park and camp overnight. The only requirement is that a town with a decent restaurant be within 20 minutes drive.

We are not the adventuresome sort who make great reading in *Outdoor Life* or *Field and Stream*. We are just ordinary people with a character defect which causes us to set aside a week's vacation for physical abuse in Canada's woodlands.

Six individuals make up the core of the canoe crew. They are: The Old Sourdough, The Cook, The Mechanic, The Ex-Marine, The Fisherman and Myself.

The Old Sourdough has been camping for as many years as I have been on this earth plus 20 more. He grew up in the Colorado Rockies and loves to spin tales of his younger days when he'd take a pack horse up into the mountains for days on end.

"That was camping. With my 30/30 Winchester in one hand and a strip of beef jerky wrapped in sourdough bread in the other, I'd skip school and hike into the foothills for the day. I learned more about nature than any school book could ever teach me," he would tell us as we sat around the campfire.

In his later years, he traded his pack horse for a family of kids who were generally less than enthusiastic about trips into the timberline. The howl of wolves was replaced with the screaming of uncomfortable kids and the nagging of a wife dragged out of her happy home.

The Old Sourdough is good to have along. Although he is not as strong a paddler as some of us and not as surefooted on the portages, he is great at making morning campfires. No matter how late the Old Sourdough stays up at night, he's always the first one up. And the first thing he does after putting in his teeth, is to start a campfire. The exercise gets his old bones moving and offers the rest of us the prospect of a warm cup of coffee.

The Cook is a chemist by trade, but you'd never believe it after watching him cook. You would think that a man of science would be precise in his cooking. Yet out in the woods, The Cook reverts to his true self— a handful of this, a scoop of that and stir it together until it resembles library paste. His philosophy on campsite cooking is: If it's hot and filling, it's good. Who cares about taste; heck, when you're starving, anything tastes good.

He is an enthusiastic cook and attentive to needs of the crew. He always serves breakfast in the morning, lunch in the early afternoon and supper just before sundown. If I were cook, or any of the other guys in the group were to play cook, breakfast would be served at noon, lunch would be a Snicker's bar and supper would be a bedtime snack. It is for that reason, no one has ever asked to take over The Cook's duties.

The Mechanic is one of those rare individuals who has a touch with anything held together with nuts, bolts, nails or screws. Give him a screwdriver and jackknife, and he can fix darn near anything. Give him a yard of duct tape, he can fix a canoe chewed up by a rock garden. He loves to talk about cars. He's the type of person who tends to talk about engines and powertrains instead of makes and models. He's great to have around when your fishing reel breaks or the campstove won't light.

The Ex-Marine is a big, powerful man. Although not accustomed to the woods, he survives on sheer strength alone. He is our Caterpillar tractor, someone who can skid a canoe through the trees with ease, lift a canoe over a beaver dam or remove a fallen tree from a portage trail. He is the person you like to take along when gathering firewood. You don't need an ax or saw, just point him toward a fallen tree and watch him break it up with his powerful arms. The only thing stronger than his back is the sound of his snoring. With him around, we never have to worry about bears invading the campsite—except if they think his snoring is the sound of some long lost relative.

The Fisherman is the type of person who doesn't pack long underwear because he needs the room for fishing gear. He is fun to have around the campfire for he tells marvelous stories involving the fish he has caught over the years. His stories are unique because the size of the fish caught is secondary to setting the scene. He loves to describe in great detail the lake he was on, the animals he encountered and the weather he experienced. He boasts how that great muskie exploded from the lily pads and fought like the devil himself before he was able to boat him. The Fisherman serves as guide for those of us who like to fish, but beyond knowing how to tie a lure to a line, know diddly about the art and science of fishing. He also serves one other valuable function. He loves cleaning fish. He is an expert at it. I've often remarked that he should have gone into medicine for he'd make a wonderful surgeon. "Think they'd let me use my fillet knife?" he once asked.

Then there is me. I am the writer, the chronicler of each and every trip. My hands aren't as tough as The Mechanic's, my back isn't as strong as The Ex-Marine's, nor is my knowledge of nature as extensive as The Old Sourdough's, but I can weave a story. I can make The Fisherman's catch any size fish he'd like or make the battle to get it as fierce as any fisherman has ever fought. I serve other functions besides writing. Because I tend to spend a lot of time napping next to the campfire, I am responsible for making sure there is always enough wood on the fire.

It is this group which each year tests itself against Canada's Curse. We have a lot fun, but for some reason we have a hard time convincing any one else to join us.

Optimism has no place in the outdoors

I hate optimistic outdoorsmen.

You know the type. You're standing in a pouring rain; there's a wind right out of the Arctic Circle, and there isn't an inch of dry clothing on your body— and he says: "Isn't it great being outdoors."

Baloney.

If I'm cold, wet and miserable, I want the whole world to know that I'm cold, wet and miserable.

To me, half the "fun" of being out in the wilderness is complaining about the weather or whatever else nature throws your way.

I'm out in the woods to get away from it all. I'm not there to smell the roses and lie in the moss. I'm there to relax and I think it's only reasonable that nature be accommodating. Let it rain on someone from Chicago.

Some people refuse to let nature get the better of them.

The Fisherman is that way.

We can be out in the canoe for hours and after nary a nibble he'll turn to me and say: "Isn't it great being outdoors. Wow, what a really beautiful lake."

"Yeah, yeah, beautiful lake," I grumble under my breath. "If I had wanted to sightsee, I would have taken the family down to Disney World. I'm here to catch fish and they aren't cooperating."

"You don't understand," The Fisherman says softly as he replaces the lure on his line. "Most of the enjoyment of fishing is being on the lake. I love to watch the waves play with the reflections of the clouds above. I like to feel the wind swirl through the pines and rip across the water."

"I'd like to see a fish, wind or no wind," I mutter as I reel in my spinner for the umpteen thousandth time. "Just a nibble, a fin breaking water... even a nanosecond of a bite...that would make me appreciate being here."

Suddenly The Fisherman looks up. "Wow! See that eagle?"

I look up. "It's a crow."

"An eagle."

"There aren't any eagles up here," I reply sharply.

"Isn't that a magnificent sight?" he continues.

"Sure, if you like crows. The girls in the swimsuit issue of *Sports Illustrated* are magnificent sights. Crows don't cut it in my book."

The tip of my pole bends. I give it a yank. It yanks back.

"Snagged!" I groan. "If I hadn't been watching that stupid eagle, uh, crow of yours. Darn! That's a $4 lure on the end of that line."

"I guess you're right, it probably is a crow," The Fisherman concedes. "But you know, if you think about it, crows are pretty neat birds. I like their sleek black feathers and the way they often glide through the sky. And they are smart birds, you got to give them credit for that."

"They're flying slimeballs." I give my pole another hard yank, but the snag holds.

"For a writer, you aren't very observant," The Fisherman says, ignoring my predicament.

"Hey, today I'm fishing. Tomorrow I'll write. Today I want to catch fish. Tomorrow I'll capture it in words." I give my pole a strong tug. The line breaks.

"Hey! Look a beaver!" The Fisherman says excitedly.

I look up. "Where?"

"Over there," he says pointing just left of the bow.

"That's a bush," I say shaking my head.

"Nah, it's a beaver, a big one at that. Why, that's the biggest beaver I've ever seen. I've got to remember to tell my wife about it."

"For crying out loud, man, it's a bush!"

"Isn't this neat. Boy, I'm glad we came out here this morning."

"So am I," I mutter sarcastically. "It's really neat being in a canoe with a guy who thinks a bush is a beaver. Geez Louise!"

I glance up at the bush once more. Suddenly a large ball of brown fur emerges from behind it, waddles out and slides into the water, its large flat tail slamming into the surface with a loud retort.

I bury my head in my tackle box.

"It's showtime!" The Fisherman yells. I look up and see his pole sharply bent and jerking side to side. A few minutes later, he pulls in a 38-inch northern.

"Isn't it great being here," he exclaims.

"Yeah." I drop my head back into the tackle box.

Fearsome fire starter fizzles

Lighting the first fire of the day is a ritual The Old Sourdough takes very seriously.

He takes great pride in being able to start a fire no matter what weather the sunrise brings. He could start a blaze in a blizzard.

I admire his skill.

I mean, just about anyone can start a fire in the middle of the afternoon on a sunny, dry day. The hardest part is finding suitable firewood. But to start a fire in the darkness before sunrise is a special talent.

No one in our canoe crew wants to take the job away from the old man. We prefer sleep to starting fires.

Sleep isn't a problem with The Old Sourdough. He can stay up past midnight and still be up and about before 6:00 a.m.

Just before daybreak he crawls out of his tent, spends a minute or two searching for his teeth and then heads for the fire ring.

He takes a stick and carefully sifts through the charred embers and half burned logs to see if anything is salvageable. He takes his time, even though the winds are chilling his hands and his frost covered boots are numbing his feet.

After clearing out the fire ring, he walks over to the woodpile, lifts off the plastic tarp and carefully selects a handful of sticks and small logs. He is careful not to pick logs too big or sticks too small. He knows the fire must build on a gradual progression from twig to little branch to big branch to log.

"Lighting a fire is like life– if you take things too fast, you and the fire will burn out," The Old Sourdough once told me.

In the cold morning air, the old man carefully builds a tiny teepee of twigs and then reaches into his back pocket and pulls out his secret firestarter. We suspect it is a mixture of dry moss and finely cut birchbark. The Old Sourdough guards it like gold.

"Why don't you try this fire starting ribbon?" the Ex-Marine once asked The Old Sourdough.

"Heck, that'll take all the fun out of starting a fire. It'd be like kissing your wife while wearing a surgical mask. The feel of fire wouldn't be there," he replied.

"I don't care diddly about the feel of fire-starting, all I know is I'm FEELING darn cold!" the Ex-Marine complained.

"If you're cold, go gather up some more firewood," The Old Sourdough replied as he gathered up kindling.

The Ex-Marine grumbled and walked off into the woods.

The Old Sourdough concedes one modern convenience. He has given up on wooden "strike anywhere" matches. "Strike anywhere, baloney," the old man once remarked. "I've lost more matches trying to ignite them on rocks than I'd care to think about. No sir, I'll flick my Bic if you please."

After igniting his secret firestarter, the Old Sourdough softly puffs on the little red glow inside the teepee of twigs. Slowly the red glow brightens and grows. The old man pauses for a moment, looks around, then turns back to the teepee and gives it hard, quick bursts of breath.

Suddenly the twigs burst into flame. Within minutes the branches are burning and the old man is putting on the logs.

The crackling sound of the fire is our alarm clock in the woods. It arouses us and we look up to see the bright orange glow across the side of the tent facing the fire. By the time we get out of our sleeping bags, the Old Sourdough has coffee on.

Once I actually awakened before The Old Sourdough. I didn't feel like going back to sleep, so I decided to try my hand at starting the morning fire.

My approach to starting a morning fire was slightly different from the old man's: To heck with the romance of fire building, I'm freezing to death and I want warmth and I want it now.

I ran over to the woodpile, scooped up several small logs and dropped them into the fire ring. Then I walked over to The Cook's area and rummaged through his gear until I found the gallon can of campstove fuel.

I doused the logs with a goodly dose of high octane fuel. It didn't bother me at the time that we could have cooked a week's worth of meals on what I had dumped on the firewood.

I quickly returned the can to The Cook's gear and stole a match from his backpack.

Now the first time I tried lighting a campfire this way, I forgot how quickly the fuel vapors rise and spread. Darn near burned off my boots when I threw that match.

A bit smarter this time, I stood many yards from the fire ring when I flicked that match.

I watched as the match gently flew toward the fire ring.

WHOOOOSH!

The concussion caved in the sides of nearby tents.

"GOOD LORD WHAT WAS THAT!" The Mechanic shouted from inside his tent.

The Old Sourdough raced out of his tent like he once charged out of the bunkers during World War II.

"Boy! You trying to get yourself killed!" he said angrily.

The Fisherman crawled out his tent which had collapsed around him. "Must have been one heckuva storm last night," he said shaking his head.

"Wasn't a storm, it was this lunkhead, pyromaniac!" The Old Sourdough growled.

"Hey, I don't know why you guys are complaining. Why just look at that fire," I said proudly.

Sure enough, in the center of the fire ring was a fire any Boy Scout would have been proud of. A nice warm fire which cut through the frosty morning air.

"You guys can complain all you want, but when Ol' Oakland turns on the thermostat, there's heat!" I continued.

"Yeah, I'll say," The Cook said scratching his head as he looked down at the melted plastic containers at his feet. "That was one firestorm you created, boy. I wonder how hot chocolate will taste mixed with melted plastic."

"Who cares about hot chocolate, look what he did to my boots," the Ex-Marine said as he picked up his boots which had been sitting about six feet from the fire ring. The laces were burned off.

"Heck, a little parachute cord will fix up your boots good as new and we've got plenty of hot chocolate in the pack," I said nonchalantly. "Minor sacrifices for waking up to a warm environment."

"Warm as a nuclear holocaust," The Mechanic said. "Take a look at yourself."

I pulled a shiny pot from The Cook's kitchen kit and looked at my reflection. My beard was an ashen white. I looked down and discovered my blue jeans had become black jeans.

"Some things are best done the old fashion way," The Mechanic said with a laugh.

Fish video evokes visions of fame

The Fisherman called it a great idea.

The rest of us weren't so enthused.

"No way! There is absolutely, positively no way you'll ever get me to carry a camcorder into Canada's wilderness," The Mechanic said emphatically.

"Come on guys, this is our chance to make some big bucks... and I'm willing to split it with you," The Fisherman said.

"How big?" The Mechanic asked skeptically.

"Mucho thousands."

"Like enough to buy that Jeep I've had my eye on?"

"And a Corvette to boot," The Fisherman said.

The Mechanic scratched the side of his head. Talking about

cars definitely aroused his interest.

"Sounds pretty risky to me," I said.

"It's a sure thing," The Fisherman said enthusiastically.

"Now run this by me again," The Old Sourdough said as he popped a can of light beer.

The Fisherman took a few steps back and raised his hands so that they formed a frame for some invisible picture.

"Sports videos are where it's at. Go into any video store and you'll see entire sections devoted to hunting and fishing videos. But I have yet to see one on *Fishing Canada by Canoe*," he said adding dramatic emphasis to the title.

"All we have to do, my friends, is film about two hours of one of our fishing forays and add a little expert commentary by your's truly," he explained.

"Expert commentary?" The Mechanic laughed.

"Hey, if I can show fish being caught– and you know we always catch fish– that is sufficient qualification as an expert. I mean, you don't need a college degree to be a fisherman."

"OK, we'll take the camcorder with us, but I am not carrying it, you hear me, I am not lugging around camera equipment. It's hard enough dragging my fishing tackle up Canada's Curse," The Mechanic said.

A couple of weeks later, we were at our campsite along the river of hurt. We had spent the last two days enduring hard portages and an unusually large number of beaver dams and logjams. Our struggles were faithfully recorded by The Fisherman's camcorder. He called it setting the stage; a number of us called it getting out of work.

"Get that thing outta my face," The Cook yelled as he pushed The Fisherman and his camcorder away.

"Hey, we've got to make this realistic. I want fishermen to believe this is authentic," The Fisherman explained.

"You want AUTHENTIC! You want REALISTIC! I'll give you AUTHENTIC!" The Mechanic shouted.

The Fisherman turned the camera toward The Mechanic

and turned it on.

The Mechanic stood up, took off his gloves and turned his palms toward the lense. "Get a shot of those blisters...beauties aren't they."

The Fisherman zoomed in on the hands.

The Mechanic then lifted up one foot, took off the boot and sock to reveal one very swollen and bruised ankle. " I got that lifting that good for nothing canoe over that last beaver dam. My foot slipped and my ankle slammed into a sharp rock," The Mechanic said speaking at the camera.

Then he turned his back to it.

"What are you doing?" The Fisherman asked with a puzzled look.

The Mechanic didn't answer. The Fisherman continued filming the Mechanic's back, not realizing that The Mechanic was quickly unfastening his belt, unbuttoning his pants and opening his zipper. Before The Fisherman could hit the pause button, The Mechanic had his pants around his knees.

"See that bruise! Get a shot of it, a real tight shot!" The Mechanic demanded.

The Fisherman was laughing so hard he forgot to shut off the camcorder, thereby recording for posterity The Mechanic's bare posterior.

"Hey, maybe there is a market for X-rated fishing videos," I interjected.

"Nude fishing!" The Cook laughed.

"Maybe *Playgirl* magazine would sponsor the video," The Mechanic said. He eyed each member of the crew then smirked. "Then again, maybe not."

The following day, the whole crew was out on the lake just north of the camp. It is a small lake, a widening in the river actually. But we like to think of it as a lake since there isn't a lake within a half day's paddle of camp.

The Fisherman positioned his boat so that the sun was at his back.

"OK you guys, let's start catching fish!" He yelled.

The Fisherman turned on the remote microphone.

"In this virgin woodlands of untapped lakes and rivers, the fishing is exciting and challenging," The Fisherman narrated as he panned the lake and our canoes.

"Northerns left undisturbed by humans for years lurk in these waters, just waiting to be enticed by the right lure..."

"I GOT ONE!" I screamed.

The Fisherman swung his camera around and then yelled to the Cook who was manning the stern. "Paddle over there quickly....but try to keep the canoe from rocking too much."

The Cook gave him a puzzled now-how-do-you-expect-me-to-do-that look as he grabbed the paddle.

The Fisherman stood in the bow like George Washington crossing the Potomoc, except ol' George didn't have a camcorder in his hands.

"Will you paddle more steadily!" The Fisherman yelled back to The Cook.

"This isn't a pontoon boat, you know!" The Cook shouted back.

Meanwhile I continued reeling in the fish. "Feels like a good sized northern!" I yelled to The Fisherman.

"Don't lose him!" The Fisherman yelled back and then turned his head toward the remote microphone. "It's man against fish as the skillful fisherman slowly brings in a trophy sized catch..." The Fisherman paused for a moment to play director.

"Hey! Can you look a little more skillful!"

"Say what?" I yelled back.

"Can you look a little more professional and a little less like a Boy Scout who just hooked his first perch!" The Fisherman shouted.

I straightened my back and lifted the pole a little higher.

"OK, look like you're working to bring this monster in," The Fisherman directed as The Cook brought the canoe alongside ours.

"I am working!"

I motioned for The Mechanic, who was sitting in the bow, to grab the net and get in position.

The Fisherman whispered to The Cook to paddle the canoe to the other side of ours so that he could get a shot of the northern exploding out of the water.

I gave my reel a couple of hard cranks.

"I see him!" The Mechanic exclaimed as he dipped the net into the water.

"Hold off!" The Fisherman screamed.

"What! Are you kidding. This fish is about to take off for Kansas," The Mechanic shot back.

"I'm not in position yet."

"Hey we don't have all day here!" I yelled.

"OK, OK, go for it!" The Fisherman shouted.

I yanked up on the pole as The Mechanic swept the net forward.

"I got him," The Mechanic announced as he lifted the fish into the canoe. He reached into the net, grabbed the fish behind the eye sockets and lifted it above his head... a monstrous northern all of 20 inches long.

"CUT!" The Cook hollered and then broke out laughing.

"Well, there will be more fish," The Fisherman said optimistically as he glanced down at the camera and noticed a little red light flashing. "Oh no!"

"What's a matter," I asked.

"I must have left the camcorder on all night. That last bit of shooting just wore down the battery. I don't have any more power," he said shaking his head.

"You mean, all you got is one lousy northern and The Mechanic's butt?" The Cook muttered.

"Afraid so."

And so ended our first and last venture into outdoor video.

The bare-bottomed boogie

When you're in the woods, the quickest way to bring civilization down on you is to take a bath.

I'm not exaggerating.

Where we canoe in Canada, you don't expect to see other people. Most people aren't into that kind of self abuse.

And we usually don't see anyone.

There are the sounds of people.

Float planes flying overhead.

Chainsaws whining in the distance.

But never any people.

That is until I decide to take a bath.

About the only way you can take a bath up there is to jump into the river. Depending on the kind of day it is and the water temperature, it can be a pleasurable or torturous experience.

I can usually go a couple of days before I need a bath, provided I don't share a tent with anyone. But there comes that time when the grime must come off.

One year, more than dirt came off.

It was a rare, sunny afternoon. The fish weren't biting so we headed back to camp. As soon as I got back, I grabbed a towel, my bottle of biodegradeable soap and headed off to a shallow bend in the river which at that moment was warmed by full sunlight.

I got to the bank, took off all my clothes except for my underpants and boots. The underpants I would use as a washcloth and my boots, which were wet to begin with, would keep my feet from being cut by the sharp rocks on the bottom.

The water was unusually warm that year. Some years, my bath lasts all of 30 seconds. This year, 20 minutes had passed and I was still splashing about.

Suddenly my eye caught a flicker of light upstream. I turned and gasped. That burst of light was the sun reflecting off the hull of an aluminum canoe.

I ducked down. I didn't think whoever was in the canoe had seen me. As they came closer, I could make out a woman in the bow and a short, stocky man in the back. They looked as if they were in their mid 30s.

The water where I was standing was only waist deep. Figuring that the underwear I was holding in my hands would be insufficient to cover what needed to be covered, I decided to make a quick sprint to the woods.

All I heard as I exploded out of the water was a female voice saying "My God! Harold, what was THAT..."

I moved so fast that my feet literally pulled from my boots which were held in a patch of mucky bottom. As I left the water, I flung my underwear into the bushes and dropped the soap bottle on the bank. Barefoot and barebottomed I ran into the woods.

You haven't lived until you have run naked through dense brush and low hanging pine branches. I felt like I had been flogged with a cat-o'-nine tails and scrubbed down with Brillo pads.

I huddled behind a stand of fern-like plants and watched as the canoe passed by. I could see the woman pointing at something in the brush and I heard the man tell her: "That's a strange portage marker. Looks like a pair of men's briefs." Then I saw the woman noticing my boots as the canoe glided over them. I was thankful the water was deep enough to deter them from fishing out the boots and taking them home as souvenirs.

The canoe rounded the bend and disappeared downstream.

For a moment I felt almost one with nature. I realized that I now knew what man would be like totally stripped of civilization. I was no longer a man, but an animal seeking survival, or at least privacy, in the harsh north country.

I looked at my legs; they were scratched and bleeding.

And then I looked at my feet and the green little plants surrounding them. I started counting leaves.

One.

Two.

Three!

"POISON IVY!"

I leaped up and took off running for the river. I grabbed my underwear from the bushes and the soap bottle from the riverbank and hit the water like a teenager at a beach. The cool water felt good against the wounds the woods had inflicted. I immediately began scrubbing my feet, which must have helped because I never did get poison ivy...that or what I had been standing in wasn't poisonous.

The experience taught me one thing: You often pay a price for privacy, even in the wildwoods.

Ah, that sunset cocktail

One of the pleasures an excursion into the wilderness offers is the sunset cocktail.

After a hard day of paddling and portaging, nothing tastes better than a shot of whiskey or strong rum. It puts you in the right mood to make supper.

When we go on our Canadian canoe trip, we always take along enough liquor to provide us with at least one sunset cocktail each day.

I always carry one flask of fine 100 proof whiskey. I buy the high octane stuff because I figure if I'm going to lug it into the wilderness, it ought to have a little kick to it. And as I discovered one year, 100 proof whiskey is great for easing the itch of mosquito bites.

It's my doomsday bottle.

Should I get run over by a canoe or mauled by a bear, I can at least dull the pain with a swig or two of potent whiskey.

After a hard day of paddling, the whiskey takes the pain away from muscles which are used to nothing more strenuous than typing and carrying file folders.

Anyway, I think I can justify the added weight of the

whiskey, even though a purist would likely argue it would be wiser to pack two more pair of socks and another pair of pants instead. They'd contend dry socks are more important than getting snockered.

I must admit, though, things have been getting out of hand during recent trips.

Take for instance the trip of '87. It was an unusually hard trip that year. The river was down. It seemed like we dragged our canoes more than paddled them. The weather was hot and humid, and the bugs were out in force.

And it seemed like the packs felt heavier that year. I figured I was just growing weaker in my old age.

After a particularly grueling first day, we all sat around the campfire complaining about everything associated with woods and rivers.

"Cocktail time," The Old Sourdough announced.

"I'll fetch the water," The Cook said as he left for the river.

One by one, we left the campfire and headed toward the packs by our tents. Soon we were all back and ready for a relaxing northwoods cocktail.

I pulled out my flask. "Anybody want some?"

"Nope," said The Old Sourdough as he pulled out his own flask.

Then The Mechanic gave a hoot and pulled out two 32-ounce cans of beer.

"Beer?" I cried out "You brought beer? Are you crazy, the stuff must weigh a ton!"

"Heck, it will be gone by tomorrow," he boasted.

Then The Fisherman opened his pack and pulled out a 3 liter box of wine and two bottles of homemade beer.

"You mean, I lugged 3 liters of wine over a half mile, rock strewn portage," I screamed.

"Hey, just because you're in uncivilized territory doesn't mean you must become uncivil. Care for a glass?"

"What next, a wet bar?" I asked sarcastically.

"Nah, we'll just carry in a quarter barrel next time," The Mechanic said.

"Not on my back!" I replied.

"Heck, we'll fly it in," The Mechanic said. "We'll just rent a plane a couple of weeks before the trip and drop a barrel with a buoy right in the middle of the lake. It will be cold by the time we reach camp."

"Can you imagine what would happen if the barrel broke upon impact?" The Cook said. "Why we'd have a lake of polluted pike."

"Hey, don't complain," The Old Sourdough said. "You'd have beer battered fish."

"Or a walleye hangover," The Mechanic added as he finished off one of the beers.

The old man poured another capful of whiskey into his cup. "Since you're flying in the beer, you might as well fly in the hors d' oeuvres... a little cheese and crackers, some shrimp, pickled herring and smoked oysters."

The Cook suddenly became wide-eyed. "Yeah, you could drop in all our provisions— we'd have steaks instead of rice and whatever-else-is-handy casseroles."

"And eggs," The Ex-Marine said wistfully. "I'd kill for two fried eggs and a slice or two of bacon."

There was a pause in the conversation as everyone reflected on the thought of bacon and eggs for breakfast. It was a lovely moment. We finished our cocktails and got back to reality... a supper of rice, canned chicken and whatever-else-was-handy casserole.

Life in the Canadian suburbs

At the base camp real estate is at a premium.

There are only a few good spots on which to pitch a tent so when our canoe crew nears the campsite, the race is on. Our canoes cut across the last stretch of water like powerboats.

At the base camp you have only two areas suitable for tents: The area immediately around the fire ring, which we call the downtown, or an area about 30 yards down a path, which we call the suburbs.

Each area can support roughly three tents. You can get a fourth tent in the suburbs if the tent's occupant doesn't mind sleeping on exposed tree roots.

Being a "yuppie" at heart, I prefer to spend my Canadian experience in the suburbs.

The suburbs are quieter. You don't have that rowdy nightlife out there because you don't have a campfire. You don't have to put up with those war stories or deer hunting tales.

You have more room in the suburbs. You don't have to feel guilty stringing a clothesline and hanging your wet pants and underwear on it.

Generally, the riffraff stays out of the suburbs, those itinerant creatures who come calling in the night and make off with whatever food you forgot to secure.

Suburban campers tend to have fewer accidents since they tend to store much of their gear in the downtown area, which is closer to the canoes. Consequently, you don't have tripping over fish poles or inadvertently putting one's foot in a fry pan resting on the ground.

There are distinct disadvantages to living in the base camp suburbs.

Like if you forget to bring your flashlight, you are in a world of hurt. There are no lights in the suburbs, no campfire light, no propane lanterns hanging from tree branches.

I once had to get up in the middle of the night because nature called, and I tried to make it without a flashlight. I walked right into The Ex-Marine's tent. The occupant of the tent thought he was being attacked by a bear and started hitting me with one of his boots. The commotion woke up the entire camp.

The other disadvantage is commuting. You might think that walking 30 yards to the downtown isn't so bad. Well, let me tell you, when you wake up in the morning and its 20 degrees outside and the boots you left outside your tent are frozen solid, the campfire being 30 yards away is a real pain. Walking barefoot down a frost covered path is no fun, particularly when traffic is bad.

Residents of the downtown, on the other hand, merely take two steps out of their tent and they're next to the fire.

Downtown residents are also closer to the food. They are right next door to The Cook's area. It's nothing for them to get up for a midnight snack. In the suburbs such an endeavor would be foolhardy.

The downtown is where the action is. There is life after sundown. In the suburbs after sundown everyone is usually sleeping or suffering adverse reactions to one of The Cook's suppertime concoctions.

Having been established by moose hunters decades ago, the downtown is older and better developed. The ground is packed and free of rocks and exposed roots. The tent sites are flat and free of debris. There are places to sit. Old 16-penny nails pounded into tree trunks offer a place to hang your gear.

The downtown is closer to the canoes which means when you first arrive or when you leave it takes less effort to carry your gear to and from the canoe, a real advantage when you have spent most of the day lugging your pack down portage trails.

There are some disadvantages to living in the downtown.

Congestion is greater. The tent sites are closer together because the room is needed for the firepit and The Cook's area.

It's louder. In addition to the commotion around the camp-

25

fire, there is a tendency for the snorers in the group to choose the downtown.

And never think that you'll be able to sleep late in the downtown. If the sound of the campfire doesn't wake you up in the morning the banging of pots and pans by The Cook and the accompanying swearing surely will.

There are two advantages both neighborhoods of tents share.

You never have to pay property tax.

And you never have teenagers racing cars down the street in the middle of the night. Just the Old Sourdough stumbling down the path in the dead of the night looking for an impromptu latrine and cursing under his breath every time he stubs his toe on a rock or root.

Make mine pecan, please

Every trip to the outdoors has its traditions.

For some people, it's a favorite wayside where they rest from a long car ride.

For some, it's a favorite roadside cafe where the steak and eggs taste good after one too many cheeseburgers to go.

For the Canoe Crew, it is The Pie Stop.

Halfway between Thessalon and Chapleau in Ontario, Canada, there is a restaurant-gas station we call The Pie Stop. For us it is the last point of civilization, the last flush toilet, before we enter the wilderness.

We usually hit The Pie Stop in early morning. Having driven all night, we are ready for a little pick me up in the form of fresh baked pie.

I'm not sure if the restaurant staff shares the same enthusiasm for us as we do for their pies. We are not what you might call big spenders.

A typical visit to The Pie Shop goes something like this...

Six of us sit down at the counter. Since we have been driving with each other all night and haven't had the opportunity to "freshen up," we sit with an empty stool between us.

"What'll you have?" the waitress asks The Old Sourdough.

"What kind of pie you have?" he replies.

"Apple, blueberry, cherry and raisin."

"No pecan?" he asks with a hint of disappointment in his voice.

"Not today."

"Then I'll have blueberry."

The waitress moves on to The Mechanic who is sitting two seats down.

"What would you like?" she asks in a voice too pleasant for that time of day.

"What kind of pie do you have?" he mumbles.

She recites the list.

"I'll have cherry."

The waitress comes up to me.

"I'll have apple."

She smiles, apparently thankful for not having to recite the list again.

She moves two stools down to The Cook.

"What kind of pie do you have?"

The waitress sighs and recites the pie menu again.

"I guess I'll just have a cup of coffee."

"Hey, I'd like coffee with my pie, too, " The Mechanic shouts from the other end of the counter.

"I'll have milk!" I exclaim.

"Coffee for me," The Old Sourdough says.

The waitress flips through her receipt pad and after a minute of frantic writing moves to the next member of our group—The Ex-Marine.

"I'll have pecan pie," he says with a broad smile.

"We don't have pecan pie," she sighs.

"I thought you said you didn't have pecan pie?" Old Sourdough inquires after catching only half the conversation.

"Not today, sir," she replies politely.

Finally she gets to the last member of our group, The Fisherman.

"I'll have apple pie with a scoop of vanilla ice cream and a glass of milk," he says.

The waitress sighs and puts away her book.

"Oh, miss! I'll have ice cream on mine, too." I say as I raise my hand.

"Hey, that sounds good. Make that two!" The Old Sourdough says.

The Cook looks up. "On second thought, maybe I will have pie. Miss, I'll have a cherry pie with ice cream.

The waitress turns to the pie case and opens the glass doors. I can see the reflection of her face in the mirrored sides of the case. The red in her cheeks isn't make up.

She takes a couple of deep breaths, takes out an apple pie and begins cutting. "Now, who wanted apple?" she asks without bothering to look at her receipt pad.

"Darn that apple pie looks good," The Old Sourdough says. "I'll think I'll have apple."

"Instead of what?" she asks, her voice having a hint of sharpness to it.

"Uh, I think cherry."

"It was blueberry," The Mechanic grumbles.

"You want ice cream?" The waitress asks.

"Are you sure it wasn't cherry?" The Old Sourdough asks The Mechanic.

"Do you want ice cream?" the waitress repeats loudly.

"Put a scoop on it, heck with the calories," The Old Sourdough says as he rubs his belly.

"That's the spirit," The Cook hollers.

Fifteen minutes later all the pies have been served. The waitress disappears into the kitchen, I suspect for a quick smoke, a cup of coffee and a recharging of her will to waitress.

She reappears, gathers up the receipts—our group is strictly dutch treat— and rings them up one by one. Our visit to The Pie Stop has ended for another year.

Halfway into the wilderness a strange thought strikes me. I turn to The Mechanic. "Say, did you happen to tip the waitress?"

"No, I thought you were going to take care of that."

I yell to The Old Sourdough who is paddling up behind us. "Hey! Did you tip the waitress?"

"Darn, I forgot."

Turns out none of us left a tip, another tradition of our noble group.

New Age camping beats boot camp

There are two ways to run a camp.

You can have a mini boot camp, or you can have an enlightened New Age camp.

If you prefer the latter concept, I suggest you don't take to the woods anyone old enough to have served in World War II. For some reason, any time they see a tent, they feel they're back in the military.

That's how our canoe crew is.

The Ex-Marine, The Cook and The Old Sourdough are all veterans and like to run the camp by the book.

Although they haven't stooped to blowing reveille at sun up, they have come mighty close. Instead of a bugle, we have The Old Sourdough stumbling around in the prelight hours of morning... "Where did I put my %&Y&^%!!! teeth." And he's followed by The Cook who makes enough racket to wake a hibernating bear as he searches in his food packs for breakfast fixings.

In our camp, breakfast is served promptly at sunrise. If you oversleep an hour, you'd miss it. I missed it once and spent the rest of the morning eating Snickers bars.

"I came up here to fish, not cook. I make a meal once, that's it," The Cook scolded.

Unlike at home, there are no leftovers in camp. The Cook is pretty good at judging how much to make. Anything leftover is promptly discarded by The Old Sourdough, who has this compulsion to wash dishes exactly three and a half minutes after he has completed his meal.

"Can't let them set around, they'll attract bears," he explained.

When it is time to leave, the canoe crew packs up with all the precision of a drill team. Within an hour, all the tents, all the gear, everything is in the canoes.

Just once I'd like to be a part of a New Age camp.

You awaken when your biorhythms are ready. Whether or not you are awake to watch the sunrise is unimportant.

If it is cold outside, you stay inside your sleeping bag until the morning sun has warmed the air to a more comfortable temperature.

There are no breakfasts, lunches or suppers.

You eat when you are hungry and when it is convenient. There's always a pot of stew on the fire so if you miss a meal it's no big deal.

The mornings are quiet. There is no cook banging on his pots and yelling: "Outta bed you women!" Instead you are awakened by the light of a new day or the singing of birds.

You are there to meditate, to relax and become one with nature.

Time is not your master; time is nearly nonexistent.

I remember on my first trip into Canada, I used to ask the

Old Sourdough what time of morning it was as I crawled out of the tent.

"About 5:30 a.m."

"5:30 a.m.!" I groaned.

"Sunrise will be in another 45 minutes, better get going the fish aren't going to wait," he said as he took a sip of coffee.

"Excuse me, I think I'll go back into my tent and die," I moaned.

In subsequent trips, I never asked the old man the time. I knew it would only depress me.

Ah, to be in a New Age camp where 10 a.m. is early.

You realize man is the only animal on this earth that is concerned about when he wakes up.

I mean, a raccoon wakes up when his body tells him to. He survives.

Why can't you adapt the same principle when you are in the raccoon's environment.

When you are in civilization, of course, you have to get up on time or else the whole darn world will come to an end. But in the woods, what difference does it make?

OK, you might not catch as many fish. Heck, where we fish we hook just as many at noon as we do at 8 in the morning.

One night I tried to convince other members of the canoe crew to try a New Age approach.

"You're lazy! That's the problem with the younger generation," the Old Sourdough said. "Why, when I was growing up on the farm..."

I sighed and listened to a 20-minute lecture on the hardships of farming.

I was going to suggest that his cows might have appreciated the extra rest, but thought I'd better not. I didn't need another 20-minute lecture. I had to get up early the next morning.

CREATIVE CANOEING CHRONICLES

Taming the Hike of Hurt

We called it our wheel of fortune.

It was going to make us big bucks.

All it had to do was survive Canada's Curse.

One thing members of our Canoe Crew universally dislike is portaging. It's a pain.

In the wilderness— as opposed to some popular "wilderness" canoe trails— portage trails are darn near nonexistent. In the true wilderness, you don't have gravel lanes as portage trails. Where we go, I've seen deer trails that are bigger.

When you have only one or two groups using a trail in a year, it tends to become grown over. Nobody comes in with a chainsaw and periodically clears away the fallen trees and brush.

Carrying a canoe through this mess is backbreaking. But that wouldn't be so bad if that was all you had to carry. Unfortunately, you also have to lug your gear.

You end up making two, sometimes three trips down the trail, each trip a real muscle straining, knee buckling hike of hurt.

The wheel of fortune would change all that— at least that's what The Mechanic assured us.

It was one summer's afternoon when The Mechanic came up with the idea of the wheel of fortune. The inspiration came while a few members of the Canoe Crew were over at the Old Sourdough's home discussing the fall trip over a few beers.

"I bet I could make a wheel which would fit under the canoe," The Mechanic remarked.

"What?" I said looking up from the topographic map.

"I was thinking the other day, I could build a wheel so that we could roll the canoe over a portage rather than carry it," he continued.

"Makes a lot of sense," The Old Sourdough said.

"In fact, I bet I could build it strong enough that we could put most of our gear in the canoe. We'd only have to make one trip over a portage trail with only half the effort."

"Why if it works, we could make a fortune!" I exclaimed as I popped the top to another can of beer.

"Now all we need is a tire," The Mechanic said.

"What kind of tire?" The Old Sourdough asked.

"I've got an old spare tire in my garage," I offered.

The Mechanic gave me a startled look. "Are you nuts! You're going to lug a radial tire all through the Canadian woods. No, it has to be something like a bike tire."

"Hey, I know where we can get one," I said.

"OK, you're in charge of getting the tire. I'll get the metal supports from work and begin the welding. I tell you, this is going to be great," The Mechanic said.

About three weeks before our canoe trip, my eldest daughter came up to me while I was reading the paper. "Daddy, the tire is missing off my bike."

"I know dear."

34

"Where is it?"

"Uh, daddy needed it for something."

"How am I supposed to ride my bike?"

"I'll only need it for a couple of weeks. You can ride your sister's tricycle."

"Dad!!"

She left the room and I went back to reading my paper.

"DONALD!"

"Yes honey," I said nonchalantly.

My daughter came racing back into the livingroom and stood a few feet away looking at me with that same smirk on her face as she shows when she knows her sister is going to get punished.

Right behind her was my wife.

"Donald how could you!"

"What?"

"I want you to put her bike tire back on her bike this minute," she said angrily.

"I was only going to borrow it," I said meekly.

"Do you realize the consequences of what you did? You'd go off to Canada for a week leaving me alone with a small child deprived of her only means of transportation. She'd drive me nuts in a day. If you don't get that tire back on the bike this afternoon, you might as well stay up in Canada!"

"All right, dear," I said reluctantly. I would have tried to explain our grand plans, but I figured she would not have appreciated them since she has never had to portage a canoe in Canada.

Because I was committed to obtaining a tire, my wife's objections forced me to quickly run down to the bike shop and buy a brand new 20-inch bike tire which I delivered to The Mechanic the following weekend.

"Gee, you didn't have to buy a new tire. This must have cost a fortune," he commented as he admired the wheel.

"I like to think of it as an investment," I replied.

"And one which will pay off handsomely. Just look at this

rig," he said proudly as he pulled out a structure of angle iron resembling a cross, with one crosspiece just long enough to reach the gunnels of the canoe at the midsection and the the other spanning the length of the canoe. Beneath the cross was a V-shaped assembly to hold the axle of the wheel.

The Mechanic took a socket wrench from his multi-drawer tool chest and slipped the wheel into the supports. It fit perfectly. "Boy I do good work," he said proudly.

A few minutes later, the Old Sourdough pulled up in his pickup truck. In the back were backpacks and other gear we normally take along on the weeklong trip.

"Ready to give it a test run?" he asked as he threw a heavy pack on the front lawn.

"We're ready!" The Mechanic said as he and I lifted the canoe onto the wheel of fortune and fastened it down with three strong rubber cords. The Mechanic then wheeled the canoe out of the garage by himself.

"Works like a charm. Why I can push the canoe with one finger!"

The Old Sourdough threw into the canoe a couple of backpacks, two paddles, a cookstove and three food cans filled with sand.

"OK, let's see if she'll work," The Mechanic said optimistically.

And sure enough, the canoe moved easily down the driveway, along the sidewalk and over the front lawn. The Mechanic then unloaded the canoe, flipped it over, released the cords and removed the wheel assembly. He then unbolted the wheel, flipped the canoe rightside up and placed the wheel and the crosspiece into the canoe.

"Packs in real nice, doesn't it," he said.

"It's a winner, no doubt about it," I remarked.

Two weeks later we were paddling up Canada's Curse approaching the first portage. Of all the portages, it is the easiest because it is the most accessible. A lot of fishermen use it during the summer months.

On its first field test, the wheel worked great. It fit on the canoe perfectly. We loaded up the canoe with a couple of backpacks and the entire cook kit, all of which must have weighed close to 50 pounds. The Mechanic and I wheeled the canoe up the portage trail to the other lake. One trip, that's all it took.

The other members of the Canoe Crew who still had to carry their canoe and gear were obviously envious. In fact, they were downright jealous after they had to make their second trip over the trail.

"Next year, we'll make one for you," The Mechanic said, then added with a laugh. "For a small fee, of course."

The second portage was tougher. Not many people traveled to the second lake because the fishing opportunities were scarce until you paddled up the river for a day.

We were confident though as we rigged up the wheel and loaded the canoe with our gear. "See you guys on the other side," I said as we pushed off down the path.

About 50 yards in, we encountered a fallen tree. Because of thick brush on either side, there was no way we could maneuver the canoe around it.

"Let's try lifting it over," The Mechanic suggested.

I took a deep breath and lifted. It weighed a ton, more than a ton. I strained and lifted with everything I had and then looked down. The wheel was barely an inch off the ground. Because of the wheel, we would almost have to lift the canoe over our heads in order for it and the wheel to clear the log.

"We'll have to unload it," I said as I let go of the canoe. The wheel hit the ground with a loud crack. I had forgotten about how the weight of the gear can stress the hull of a fiberglass canoe designed to float in water not air.

"No sweat, we'll just unload the canoe, lift it over and put the gear back," The Mechanic said. "We'll still save a lot of time."

And that's what we did. It worked well, and as The Mechanic had predicted, it didn't take much time. We were still ahead

37

of the others.

The trail began to gradually slope upward. Although the wheel continued to roll nicely, pushing it up the hill became harder and harder.

"Push!" The Mechanic yelled as he leaned back and pulled the bow with every bit of strength in his legs and shoulders. "I am, I am," I said as my feet slipped and my face struck the side of the canoe.

I got up and commenced pushing again. Inch by inch, the canoe rolled up the hill. Finally we reached the top and we collapsed into the brush on both sides of the trail. "Boy, what a workout," I said as I rubbed my aching thighs.

"Well, at least going down the hill is going to be a piece of cake," The Mechanic said as he got to his feet.

Slowly we pushed the canoe onto the downside of the hill. The canoe rolled like it was featherlight. "This is more like it," The Mechanic said.

Unfortunately the farther down the hill we got, the faster the canoe rolled.

"This is great!" The Mechanic yelled as he started to run along side the careening canoe.

The trail then dipped into a marshy area at the foot of the hill. The instant the wheel hit the muck, all forward motion stopped. It was as if the canoe had hit an invisible brick wall. My groin slammed into the stern of the canoe while The Mechanic fell headfirst into the mud.

My body went limp and collapsed over the end of the canoe.

"You all right?" The Mechanic said as he picked himself out of the mud.

"I'll live," I groaned. "But don't expect a lot of strong paddlin' for the rest of the day."

We looked down at the wheel. It was half buried in mud. We got on each end of the canoe and rocked it, but the wheel refused to budge. In fact, with each effort, the wheel sank deeper.

"Let's unload it," The Mechanic said with a hint of disappointment and frustration in his voice.

"Where?" I asked.

We were surrounded by smelly marsh muck. Anything dropped on it would instantly become wet and muddy.

"We'll have to carry it out," The Mechanic said as we watched the other members of our party walk past with their packs.

"Having trouble, boys," The Fisherman said with a smile.

We unloaded the canoe and carried the gear to the end of the portage and then went back for the canoe.

Normally, we'd flip the canoe over and carry it with the gunnels resting on our shoulders. But we couldn't do it that way because we had the wheel of fortune along. That forced us to carry the canoe right side up, which after a few yards became a royal pain because the keel kept digging into shoulders.

It was also a lot harder to carry because we couldn't get a good grip on it. Twice the canoe rolled off our shoulders and slammed into the ground.

"I've had enough," The Mechanic grumbled as the canoe slipped off his shoulder for the third time. "Let's put the wheel of fortune off to the side and carry the canoe the rest of the way."

I agreed and we tossed the wheel into the brush.

By the time we got to the end of the portage, the others were long gone. Ahead of us was one last portage, longer and more hilly than the first two.

The Mechanic and I looked at one another and shrugged. We loaded up the canoe and pushed off into the lake leaving the wheel of grief behind.

Giving a fish freedom is fishy indeed

"You expect me to believe that?" The Cook said incredulously.

"Sure," I replied.

The Cook motioned for The Ex-Marine to come over. "You have to hear this one. Our boy here says while we were all out fishing, he caught a 40-inch northern, brought it back to camp and staked it on a stringer a couple feet off shore. And then he decided to let it go!"

The Ex-Marine looked at me as if I had just announced I had given away all my worldly possessions, traded my three-piece suit for a toga and decided to live in a tree house with a small, stuffed bear.

"No man in his right mind would let such a fish go," he said.

"Why not?" I replied.

"Well, for one thing, no one in their right mind is ever going to believe you caught such a fish in the first place."

"Take my word for it."

The two men laughed heartily.

"Look guys, we have been out here for four days now. We have eaten fish for four days...fish for supper, fish for lunch... I wouldn't be surprised if you guys served fish for breakfast tomorrow.

"Quite frankly, I'm getting tired of eating it..."

The two men looked at each other and shrugged their shoulders. I continued.

"OK, the trout was excellent the first day and great the second day, but by the third supper, the trout started losing its appeal. That first walleye fillet was out of this world. But I've been eating walleye for three days now. In fact, I'm getting to the point where I can't tell what kind of fish I'm eating. Every supper is a smorgasbord up here. Like last night, you guys weren't sure if The Fisherman and I would be bringing fish back to camp, so you went and made a pot full of beans.

"Well, we came back with one good sized northern, two walleye and a brookie. You felt a certain obligation to cook them since we had spent all afternoon and paddled halfway to the Arctic Circle to get them.

"So that night, I had three kinds of fish on my plate surrounded by a circle of baked beans..."

"OK, so it wasn't one of my best suppers," The Cook interrupted.

"Prisoners on Devil's Island had it better," I shot back.

"Anyway, earlier this afternoon, The Mechanic and I were fishing that pond to the north when all of a sudden I hooked onto what I thought was a big log," I continued.

"Turned out to be a pretty good sized northern which I spent the next five minutes fighting. I must admit, it was a real rush boatin' that baby.

"Well, we didn't have any further luck, so we headed back to camp, this big lunker dangling along side the canoe. I figured he was dead for sure.

"We got back to camp, and being a tad bit lazy, I decided to clean the fish after I had taken a nap. With the rest of you guys off fishing, it was one of the few times I could take an undisturbed siesta.

"I went down to the lake and untied the stringer from the canoe. I walked 10 feet off shore, drove a branch into the bottom and tied the stringer to it. The big northern was almost motionless. He wasn't dead, but he was getting there. Then I returned to camp to take my well-deserved nap.

"When I awakened, I grabbed my fillet knife and headed toward the lake. When I got to where I had staked out the fish, I found he had perked up considerably. Although he was swimming around, he didn't have the strength or smarts to escape.

"I stared down at the magnificent fish and started thinking

41

about having to eat him and the possibility that you guys might come back with a canoe full of fish.

"Well boys I couldn't do it. I couldn't kill that fish knowing that I really didn't need to eat him. I bent down, grabbed him along the backside, removed the stringer from his jaws and released him."

The Cook's eyes widened.

"You mean, you released him here!"

"Yeah."

"Whereabouts exactly?"

"Just off the bow of that canoe," I said pointing to my green canoe.

The Cook ripped off his apron, grabbed his pole and took off for his canoe.

"I bet he's still around and hungrier than all heck!"

"Come on, give the fish a break!" I shouted.

"No way!" The Cook said as he grabbed a paddle.

Two hours later The Cook was still fishing about 50 yards off shore and nary a nibble.

I felt pretty good.

Walkman not welcome in camp

I could tell The Old Sourdough was upset.

"That thing has no place in this camp!" He said angrily.

I didn't look up from the fire.

"You hear me, boy!"

I continued to watch the flames.

The Old Sourdough motioned to The Cook to give me a

poke in the ribs.

"Huh?"

"The old man's talking to you," The Cook said.

"Huh?"

I lifted the tiny headset from my ears and turned off the small stereo tape player I was holding in my lap.

"The old man's talking to you," The Cook repeated.

I looked up at The Old Sourdough. His face was as red as the flames of the campfire.

"That thing has no place here," he said sternly.

"What thing?"

"That radio."

"What radio?"

"That radio," he said pointing at my tape player.

"Oh, you mean my casette player."

"Whatever," he said flatly.

"I was just listening to an REO..."

"The woods and rock n roll don't mix," he interrupted. "You come here to get away from that. Why the next thing you know, you guys will be bringing a portable TV with you."

"No way," I shot back. "You'll never catch me portaging a TV. I don't care how small it is."

The Cook and The Mechanic nodded their heads.

"You guys don't understand. You come up here to enjoy the sights and sounds of nature, the birds singing, the beavers slapping their tails on the water, the...

"The Ex-Marine swearing when his boot slips between two sharp rocks as he drags his canoe through a rock garden," The Cook interjected with a laugh.

"When I went into the Rockies, I went to sleep each night to the sound of the wolves' lullaby..."

"What were they singing– "Rock a bye baby AHoooooooooooo!" I howled as I raised my head like a wolf howling at the moon.

"And on real quiet nights, we would gather around the

43

campfire and Uncle Ted would pull his harmonica out of the saddle bag and we'd sing cowboy songs."

"That probably shut the wolves up," The Ex-Marine remarked.

"You aren't suggesting we..." The Fisherman said glancing nervously at the rest of us.

"Sure, why not," The Old Sourdough replied.

I shook my head. "Hey, I don't know about the rest of you, but hearing you guys sing, well, it'd give me nightmares for sure. I mean, you're not Gene Autry and we're not exactly the Sons of the Pioneers."

"Heck, his snoring is better than my singing," The Cook said pointing to the Ex-Marine.

The Ex-Marine glared at The Cook and then turned to The Old Sourdough.

"Maybe it would be kind of fun," he said.

"Come on, give the poor beasts of the forest a break. You'd probably scare every bear within a half mile of here. They'd probably be so shook up they'd refuse to hibernate over winter. You'd give the poor moose conniption fits," I said.

"Not to mention the fish," The Fisherman added.

"Come on guys, just one verse of 'She'll Be Coming Around the Mountain,'" The Old Sourdough said as he raised his arms like a backwoods Mitch Miller.

The guys got up and walked away from the campfire. I put my headphones back on.

That was the last time the old man ever mentioned turning our group into a camp choir.

Actually I don't see anything wrong with carrying a personal cassette player into the outdoors.

Now boom boxes are a different story.

In my opinion, the best way to turn off a boom box in the woods is with a 12-gauge shotgun. Boom boxes are as obnoxious as their owners.

It's one thing to play something that only you can hear. It's

44

quite another thing to play something that everyone within 100 yards has to live with.

Ever notice that people with boom boxes never play classical music.

You never hear New Age music in a state park campground.

Even Top 40 stuff is rarely heard.

What fills the campgrounds is heavy metal, groups which come up with the most god-awful music imaginable. It's so bad, that in the fall the darn stuff knocks leaves off trees.

I bet the state forests are filled with neurotic squirrels who inadvertently got too close to someone's boom box. The poor things probably go home at night and bang their heads against the side of the tree trying to get the ringing out of their ears.

Music has always had a place in the outdoors.

Girl Scouts will always sing campfire songs as they roast their marshmellows.

Boy Scouts will always blow reveille at sunrise.

And I'll always hum Volga Boatman as I paddle up Canada's Curse.

But I draw the line at boom boxes and sanctioning any attempt to turn our canoe crew into a camp choir. I respect the balance of nature too much.

Northwoods snack attack

Ever notice how much better food tastes when served in the woods. Sitting by a campfire, I'll consume great quantities of culinary concoctions I'd never touch at home.

Some say it is the fresh air that enhances the taste of food. Others contend that when starvation is the alternative, anything tastes great.

Our camp cook is a nice enough fellow until you get him anywhere near a cookstove. He hardly ever follows recipes and tends to measure nutritional values in pounds per square inch.

He makes this rice-tomato soup casserole that is so heavy that when he dishes it out you'd better have both hands on your plate, else the food will send it straight to the ground.

Suppertime around our campfire is usually a quiet and peaceful time. Of course, there was that time when a hot ember found its way into the bottom of The Mechanic's boot. When his barefoot slid into that boot, he shot up like some crazed Karate Kid and danced around the fire like a turbo-charged punk rocker. He yanked off the boot and plunged his barefoot into my plate of rice-tomato casserole. To his amazement, it killed the pain almost instantly.

Breakfast is altogether different.

The Old Sourdough, who spent his youth traipsing through the Colorado Rockies, believes a day at camp begins at four in the morning. He gets up, makes a cup of coffee (his idea of breakfast), then banging a stick against a fry pan, he yells out— "OK, boys let's get going, we have a full day's hike ahead of us."

Given the lack of daylight, freezing temperatures and boots drenched with dew, we usually can only summon enough ambition to make a quick cup of lukewarm coffee and spoon down a bowl of half cooked instant oatmeal.

That's why we tend to snack a lot while camping.

I usually finish off a couple of Snickers bars before mid-morning. But that's nothing compared to The Mechanic.

"Geez, how can you eat that stuff," I once asked him as he finished off a one pound bag of trail mix.

"Beats carrying it," he replied as he peeled open a package of string cheese.

Once I watched him pull from his backpack three quart-size bags of trail mix, two pounds of dried pineapples, a bag of jelly beans, a jar of beef jerky, three packages of jumbo Milky Way bars, four packs of licorice sticks, a tub of peanut butter, a box of crackers, one six-pack of beer, a flask of Jack Daniel's best, a small package of prunes and a box of bran flakes.

"It's hard keeping regular out here, if you know what I mean," he said with a hint of embarrassment.

Occasionally he forgets what all he has for provisions. Like the time he forgot about those two bananas he had packed. It took two days of hanging in a tree to air out the pack.

"Hey, it kept the mosquitos away from camp," he said later.

"Yeah, and every living thing within a 100 yards of our campsite," I replied.

"Well, how about the time you forgot about that jelly doughnut your wife had packed," The Mechanic countered. "It was so hard you could darn near sharpen your knife with it."

"But you gotta admit, it was great for driving in tent stakes," I said as I finished off my last Snickers bar.

Fish fights flourish with these fishermen

It's a good thing we go after fish rather than gold when we go canoeing.

Otherwise we'd surely kill one another.

We're all a bunch of claim jumpers. As fishermen we lack the patience to find our own fish; we'd much rather let someone else find the hot spot then mooch off their action.

A fishing excursion along Canada's Curse typically goes like this...

Three canoes cut through blue/white veils of fog draped between the dew ladened trees overlooking the banks of the silently flowing river.

Quietly, the canoeist enters a widening in the river which

becomes a small lake ringed with weed beds.

"This looks promising," The Fisherman whispers.

We all nod.

The Fisherman quickly surveys the lake and then motions to The Old Sourdough and The Ex-Marine to paddle to a weed bed on the lefthand side of the lake and then directs The Mechanic and me to head for a shallow area at the opposite end of the lake. The Cook and The Fisherman move to the righthand side of the lake.

We paddle very slowly as we cross the little lake, our canoes moving so smoothly the bows hardly create a wake. We are bound and determined to successfully sneak up on the fish this time.

As we reach our spots, we quietly get out our tackle and rig up our poles. We don't talk; we don't rock the canoe. We're like commandoes preparing for a surprise attack.

All is quiet.

All is still.

Things are so peaceful you can hear the wings of a duck flying overhead.

Minutes pass.

An hour passes.

No one has had a bite.

All that you see and hear are the lures hitting the water or an occasional groan or obscenity as someone hooks a weed.

Suddenly a wild splashing sound streaks across the lake like a clap of thunder. I stand up and look across the lake. The Cook has a fish on the line. Although he is on the opposite side of the lake, I can tell The Cook has hooked a big Northern.

"Cookie's got one!" I yell back to The Mechanic, who has already thrown his rod onto the bottom of the canoe, grabbed a paddle and thrust it into the water. I fall backward into the canoe as his first stroke lurches the canoe forward.

I pick myself up and scramble back onto the seat. I quickly grab a paddle.

"Hurry!" I yell as my paddle slaps the water, each stroke splashing water into the stern. "The old men are on the move," I shout, referring to The Old Sourdough and The Ex-Marine.

Sure enough, the two old men had also noticed The Cook's fish and they're just as quick as we younger fellows in getting their paddles in the water.

The Cook is too busy reeling in his fish to notice the two canoes converging on him like Olympic sprinters. "Hurry up, we've got company," The Fisherman shouts to his partner.

The Cook cranks the reel and yanks the fish aboard just as The Old Sourdough and The Ex-Marine slam into the side of the canoe, knocking The Cook to his knees and making him loose his grip on the big fish.

"Geez!" The Cook curses as he dives for the fish wildly thrashing about in the bottom of the canoe.

"Ease up!" The Fisherman cautions as he tries to steady the violently rocking canoe.

Moments later we pull up parallel to their canoe, which has now become steady since it is tightly wedged between our canoe and the Old Sourdough's.

"How big is it?" The Mechanic asks The Cook.

"What were ya using?" The Old Sourdough asks as he fumbles for his tacklebox.

"A daredevil," The Cook replies as he puts a 42-inch Northern on the stringer.

Instantly four other fishermen rifle through their tackleboxes for anything resembling a daredevil. The once quiet lake becomes alive with voices, slamming tackleboxes and the commotion of canoe hulls banging up against one another.

Within a few minutes the canoes drift apart so that they are floating on the edge of an imaginary circle maybe 20 yards across. The water inside the circle is alive with lures.

"GOT ONE!" I yell. "A big one by the feel of it."

I give the pole a sharp yank.

"GOT ONE, TOO!" The Ex-Marine announces.

"This fish has some weight to it," I say as I watch the tip of my pole bend toward the water.

"This isn't a minnow," The Ex-Marine says excitedly.

Suddenly in the center of the circle two entangled lures shoot out of the water like a submarine missile and hang in the air suspended between my pole and The Ex-Marine's pole.

After the laughter has died down, we decide the center area is too crowded so we all turn our attention to the waters on the other side of the canoes, all of us except The Mechanic, who has lost patience with his daredevil strategy and is now fishing with a yellow jig in the center of the circle of canoes.

Suddenly his pole whips over, its tip just touching the water.

"Feels like a walleye," The Mechanic says as he begins to crank the reel.

Even before the fish breaks water, The Cook, The Old Sourdough and I have swiftly reeled in our lures and are back into our tackleboxes looking for anything resembling a yellow jig.

As The Mechanic pulls the small walleye out of the water, The Cook and I cast our jigs into the center area between the canoes.

Minutes later, The Cook pulls out a walleye. I reel in my jig and this time cast it within inches of where his had been.

"Hey!" The Cook objects.

I smile. "Take your case to *People's Court*."

The Cook grumbles a bit and drops his jig next to the boat. Within seconds he has another strike. He looks up and gives me a smile of revenge.

"LOOK OUT!" The Ex-Marine yells as a bright yellow jig flies past The Cook's face and plops into the water next to his canoe.

"HEY!"

"What a cast," The Ex-Marine says proudly. "I thought it was going to go in the canoe for sure. That's precision casting, I tell you."

The Cook grumbles a curse or two and turns his attention to the walleye he had just caught.

I tell you, there is no chivalry among these fishermen.

Louganis of the logjams

I never thought I would need the skills of a log rolling lumberjack on a canoe trip.

But there I was precariously perched on a free floating log in the middle of a Canadian river. I knew that at any moment the log might turn, and I'd be playing log roller.

Where we canoe, logjams are common. It's mother nature's way of humbling you.

In the spring, the high waters rip roots from banks causing long, lean pines to go for a swim. And what the rains miss, the beavers take care of. Even if they are unsuccessful at building a dam– a rare event– they manage to put a lot of wood into the waters.

The trouble with logjams is that they are deceptive. You think threading a canoe through the limbs and logs would be easy. That's what I thought one brisk morning two day's paddle up Canada's Curse.

"Just push the bow toward that log," I said to The Mechanic as we slowly approached a logjam that, conservatively, looked 50 yards long.

"I think we ought to portage," The Mechanic replied.

"Nah, we can make it," I said as I stood in the canoe and surveyed the crisscrossing tangle of timber. Even if I had thought the logjam was impassable, I still would have suggested we try. You see, I hate portaging. I hate unloading canoes which I so carefully packed in the early morning hours. I hate carrying a heavy pack and paddles down trails a rabbit couldn't follow. I hate trying to thread a canoe through narrow stands of pine only to wedge the bow between tree limbs.

"I don't know," The Mechanic said skeptically.

"Piece of cake," I shot back as the bow of our canoe bumped up against a log maybe a foot in diameter. "I'll just get out on this log and pull the canoe over."

I got out onto the log, and holding onto the canoe, easily pulled half of it over the timber. My weight and that of the canoe pushed the log about three inches underwater, giving the canoe enough float to slide over it. I maneuvered the canoe along side the log and stepped in. "See, nothing to it."

The rest of the group followed.

Soon our canoes were in the middle of the logjam, the end was merely a half dozen downed trees away.

"A few minutes and we'll be through it," I yelled as I lifted my leg over the gunnel and carefully placed my boot on a thick pine log which extended out from the bank. I put a little weight on my foot. The floating tree didn't budge. I lifted my other leg over the side of the canoe and put my other foot on the log. Then I lifted myself out of the canoe.

As I was about to turn around, my right boot slipped slightly causing me to lose my balance and inadvertently push the canoe away. The canoe floated across a little gap in the logjam and wedged the bow between two big logs.

"Hey! Get over here!" I cried out to The Mechanic as I stood on the log, my arms outstretched like the pole of a highwire walker.

"Hang on, I can't get the bow free," The Mechanic yelled back.

I heard a dull cracking sound. Suddenly the log I was standing on broke free of another log holding it up.

"OOOOOOOOH!" I cried as the log drifted out into the gap between the two piles of logs. I could feel the log shifting side to side and slowly sinking from my weight.

"Hurry, I'm going down!" I yelled to The Mechanic.

Still trapped in between branches, The Mechanic threw up his arms and turned toward me. "Here, this may help," he yelled as he threw me his paddle. "Use it as a balance just like a tightrope walker would."

"Are you nuts!" I yollered as the paddle flew toward my face. I reached up and grabbed it just before it hit my nose. Unfortunately, the sudden motion shifted my weight causing the log to begin to roll.

"AAAIIIIIIEEEEEE"

Instead of coming to my aid, my buddies just sat in their canoes, sort of half-shocked, half-amused.

Moments later the paddle shot high into the air as my left foot flew off the log in one direction, and my right leg flew off in the opposite direction. In an instant, I was completely airborne. My body bounced once on the spinning log and then hit the water with a huge splash.

The next thing I remembered was a hand grabbing the collar of my coat and pulling me up alongside a canoe.

"You ought to try out for the lumberjack olympics," The Ex-Marine said as he pulled me into his canoe.

The Cook sat laughing in his canoe about 10 yards behind us. "I think we ought to start calling you the Greg Louganis of the Northwoods," he laughed.

"Come on, are we going to sit here all day," said The Fisherman, who was manning the stern of The Cook's canoe.

"All right, just a second," The Cook replied as he tried to regain his composure. He grabbed a branch and pulled the canoe against a fallen pine. Carefully he got out and turned around to grab hold of the canoe."We'll show Oakland how it's done," The Cook laughed. He lifted the bow onto the half sunken log and began to slide the canoe across the slimy wood.

As the log passed under the midpoint of the canoe, The Fisherman got up and started to move forward. He knew that in order to get a canoe completely over the log, both occupants must be outside of the canoe otherwise it would be too heavy.

The Fisherman climbed over the packs and stepped out onto the log on the side of the canoe opposite from The Cook. "OK, on three..." The two men grabbed the gunnels and took a deep breath. "One...two...THREE"

CRACK!

Instantly the big log split in two. The Cook and The Fisherman glanced up at each other, grimaced, then slid into the water and disappeared. The Cook surfaced first, grabbed the canoe and pulled himself out of the water. Unfortunately, he put too much weight on it and the canoe shifted violently to one side, throwing all the contents overboard just as The Fisherman surfaced.

Sopping wet, The Fisherman, The Cook and I pulled our canoes over to the mucky bank. As we sunk up to our knees in slime, we lifted the canoes and our gear onto land.

"Piece of cake, eh" The Old Sourdough muttered as he lifted his pack to his shoulder and set out through the thick brush. "Funniest darn cake I have ever seen."

A fool and his firewood are soon parted

"Anyone want to help me get some wood for the fire?" I asked the rest of the canoe crew.

Two shook their heads, one disappeared into his tent and two pretended to be napping.

Their reaction was understandable. My reputation for wood gathering is not the best. I don't know if I'm just clumsy or unlucky, but when I get a saw in my hands I'm darn right dangerous.

It all began five years ago. We had just arrived at the base camp. "After we set up, you and you go get some logs for the fire," The Old Sourdough said pointing to The Mechanic and me, the two youngest in the group.

After setting up my tent, I grabbed the saw and headed off into the woods. The Mechanic joined me a few minutes later just as I was about to saw down a six-inch thick pine.

"Hey are you crazy!" he yelled.

"What's a matter?"

"You don't cut down a live tree!"

"Why not? Look how straight its trunk is. Why I bet we could get two night's fire out of it."

"You ever try to burn a freshly cut log?"

"No."

"Can't do it unless you put it in a bonfire. Use fallen trees that are dried out. Like that one over there," he said pointing to a fallen tree that was resting against a live one. "The wood will be good because it hasn't been rotting on the ground. Go cut that one."

"Anything you say," I said brightly.

I walked over to the fallen tree and began sawing about a foot from its exposed roots. It was about four inches in diameter and easy to saw. Within a minute, the saw blade was through the trunk. But the tree didn't move. The top branches were hung up in the branches of nearby trees. I put down the saw and gave the old tree a push.

Meanwhile The Mechanic was about 20 feet from me picking up loose branches and was unaware of my struggle with the stubborn tree.

"OK, you no good hunk of dead wood," I said under my breath as I took a few steps backwards. Then I charged the tree like a football player attacking a blocking sled.

CRACK

Suddenly the dead tree broke loose from the branches and started falling with me hanging on.

"TIMMMMMBER!"

The Mechanic looked up just in time to see the tall tree coming down on him. The trunk of the tree came within four inches of his boots and landed on the log he was standing on, a log resting up against a large rock. What happened next was sort of like a kid jumping on one end of a teetertotter.

"AAAAAAARGH!"

The Mechanic flew off the log, did a sort of sideways backflip and landed in the pile of branches.

"You all right?" I said after I had picked myself off the ground.

"OOOOOOOHHHH!" he groaned. He got to his feet, rubbed his back and legs and then walked away. "You're dangerous, man," he said as he left.

I went back to the downed tree and sawed it in half. I attached the saw to my belt and bent over to pick up one of the pieces of trunk.

Like a weightlifter, I cleaned and jerked the heavy eight foot section of trunk onto my shoulders. I was proud of myself. It's a lot easier carrying one big piece then a pile of little logs, I said to myself.

I turned to walk down a hill toward the trail leading back to camp. Halfway down the hill, I had to turn to get around a tree. But when I turned, I didn't see one end of the log I was carrying slam up against another tree. The log shook like a bat hitting a concrete post. Suddenly I found myself losing my balance. I whipped around to catch myself, but unfortunately the other end of the trunk hit another tree and abruptly stopped. My neck hit the log like a kid being highlined by a clothesline. Down I went, the trunk falling across my chest.

The Mechanic and The Cook came running down the trail. They reached me just as I was lifting the dead tree trunk off my body.

"You OK?" The Cook asked.

I assured him I was fine.

"The saw isn't," The Mechanic said picking up two pieces of blade. "You must have fallen on it."

I looked down at my brand new chamois shirt. A section of it was chewed to heck by the saw.

"You're dangerous," The Mechanic sighed and walked away.

I guess my problem is I'm too lazy to make two trips. I got into trouble one other time for that reason.

It was getting close to dark when we paddled up to this rather undeveloped campsite. It was located in a marshy area so there wasn't any nearby firewood. The closest source of firewood was on a hillside across the river.

"I'll go get us some wood," I said as I motioned to The Fisherman to come along. We jumped into a canoe and paddled to the otherside.

"You have the saw?" The Fisherman asked looking around the bottom of the canoe.

"Darn, I knew I forgot something," I said as I kicked the side of the canoe.

"No matter," I said. "There's enough fallen stuff we won't need to cut anything."

Sure enough, the hillside had never been touched by anyone. Fallen trees and branches abounded. Within 15 minutes we had a pile of branches three feet high and six feet long.

"How are we going to get all that wood back to camp?" The Fisherman asked.

"Simple," I said confidently. "We'll just take this rope, feed it under the pile, bring it up and around the branches and tie it tight." I explained as I worked with the rope. After tying the last knot, I walked over to a long, straight branch about two inches in diameter and picked it up. "Now all we do is push this through the top of the pile and under the rope. Then you put one end on your shoulder and I'll put the other end on my shoulder. Won't be any worse than portaging a canoe."

I got the idea from watching Tarzan movies as a kid. The natives used the same technique to carry ivory tusks out of the forbidden elephant graveyard. I figured what worked for ivory would work for a pile of logs. And it did. We got that entire pile of wood back to the canoe with ease. The Fisherman waded out next to the canoe and then we rolled the pile into the center of the boat.

"How about that! A whole day's worth of firewood in just one trip," I said proudly.

The Fisherman stepped into the bow of the canoe and I got into the stern and pushed off.

"I don't know about this," The Fisherman said nervously as

he slowly put his paddle into the water.

The canoe did feel unusually wobbly. "Must be the pile is a bit high centered. I'll just lower our center of gravity by kneeling down," I said as I lifted myself off the seat.

The next thing I remember was being completely submerged in icy water.

When I got back to the surface I saw The Fisherman clinging to the side of the capsized canoe. The pile of firewood was floating about 20 yards downstream.

"They warned me about you," The Fisherman said as his hands slipped off the canoe's hull and he once again slipped beneath the surface of the water.

His head popped out of the water and he grabbed for the canoe again.

"You're dangerous," he groaned as he spit river water from his mouth.

Ever since that fateful swim, no one from the canoe crew will volunteer to collect firewood with me.

Canada's Curse is hard on cameraman

Being the camp cameraman is challenging at times.

"Oak, you gotta get a picture of this," The Fisherman yells as he runs into camp, a stringer of walleye flapping at his side.

"No way!" I shout back.

"Why not?"

"It's pouring rain!"

"So what?"

"So, cameras don't like rain. The surest way to kill a camera is to get it wet."

"Oh, put it in a plastic bag and get out here," The Fisherman says.

"Are you nuts? All it takes is one drop in the right place, one bead of water inside the case and the shutter will shutdown. I could buy you a new canoe for what it would cost me to replace my camera."

The Fisherman grumbles and walks away.

Such conversations occurred during my early visits to the Canadian Curse. That's when I used to take my expensive 35mm SLR camera and lens. I had visions of capturing beautiful pristine woodland scenes which I could frame and hang in my den and livingroom.

I realized the risk and took what I thought were adequate precautions.

Like the first time I went on the trip, I didn't carry a camera bag. I carried a metal ammo box which I had purchased from the local army surplus store. Although the clerk assured me that it was waterproof, I had to find out for myself. One night I unrolled a couple yards of tissue paper, wadded it up into a loose ball and put it inside the ammo box. Then I took the box into the basement and put it in one of the washtubs. Then I placed a brick on top of it and filled the tub with enough water to immerse the box.

One hour later I returned, opened the box and found absolutely dry tissue paper. I mean, had there been any moisture whatsoever, it would have revealed itself on the fragile tissue.

Off to Canada I went confident that my camera would survive the wilderness and all that mother nature could throw at us.

Unfortunately, I failed to take into account how heavy an ammo box becomes after you have carried it and a canoe for 300 yards. After the first portage, I felt sure my right arm was longer than my left.

I also discovered that having the ammo box along did not guarantee the camera would stay dry. That realization came with the first picture.

60

"Will you watch it!" I yelled.

The Mechanic, who was in the bow of the canoe, turned around and gave me a puzzled look.

"What's wrong?"

"You just got my camera wet. I wanted to get a picture of those pine trees over there so I took my camera out of the ammo box and was about to shoot when you decided to paddle. Your first stroke was so hard it sent a curtain of water flying back into the stern!" I explained.

"Sorry."

I quickly dried the camera off with my shirt and was about to put it back into the ammo box when I noticed that the padding inside was all wet. The spray from the paddle not only got me and my camera wet, but also drenched the interior of the box!

Then there was the time I nearly took my $700 camera and lens for an impromptu bath.

Because I was "the expedition photographer," I was obligated to record for posterity our struggles through anything resembling whitewater. I didn't mind because it meant I didn't have to A) exhaust myself paddling around rocks and B) get myself wet when paddling around rocks was less than successful.

"Let me out here," I said motioning to The Mechanic to paddle to the left hand bank just ahead of a stretch of rapids.

After I got to shore, I yelled to the rest of our party: "Hold up a minute while I get into position." I then went traipsing through the worst tangle of brush and fallen trees I had ever experienced. What made matters worse was every time I took a step, that darn ammo box slammed into the side of my knee.

Swearing all the way, I worked my way downstream until I reach the midpoint of the rapids. Then I cut back toward the river.

I broke through the brush, slid down a muddy bank and crashed knee deep into the water. When I got up, the ammo box was no longer in my hand. I looked into the muddied water, but couldn't see it. It was at that moment I discovered another disadvantage of ammo boxes. They sink.

61

I moved my foot around in the water until I felt the box. I pulled it out of the water, opened the lid and found a perfectly dry camera. I congratulated myself on my forethought and then proceeded to walk across the large boulders which formed the outer edge of the rapids.

"OK guys, come on down," I shouted.

The Old Sourdough and The Cook were first down the chute.

I looked through the lens.

"Darn, I'm too far away," I said to myself.

I put the camera's strap around my neck and then jumped to a large boulder about three feet away. My landing was perfect, but the momentum caused the camera to swing out from my body and then swing back with all the force of a left hook to the stomach. The sharp pain caused me to grab my midsection and nearly fall off the rock.

"Hey get a shot of this!" The Old Sourdough yelled from the bow of the canoe which was heading my way.

I quickly checked my f-stop, advanced the film and put the viewfinder to my eye. All I saw was a blurred imaged of a canoe barreling down on me.

"LOOOOOOK OUT!" The Sourdough screamed.

I took the camera away from my face just in time to see the canoe slam into the side of the boulder I was standing on. The impact shook the rock and my balance.

"OOOOOOOH NOOOOO!"

One leg went west, one leg went east and one butt went due south, right on top of the rock. It felt like a punter had just kicked me right between the uprights. I rolled off the rock and into the water.

For a moment, the only thing above water was my right hand which had a death grip around the camera.

Today I don't take chances like that. I carry into Canada a cheap 35mm fixed focus camera. Cheap cameras can survive the elements.There's nothing to them: a case, a plastic lens, a shutter and knob to advance the film. Heck, you can deep six one of those suckers and she'll still take good pictures.

When all they want you to take is pictures of dead fish, the $19.95 special will do just fine.

Saucers among the stars

One of the neat things about the remote woodlands of Canada is the stars.

I know a few astronomers who'd kill for the view of the night sky I see as I lay on the bottom of my canoe as it drifts across a still, black, Canadian lake.

The Milky Way isn't a picture in a book. Up there it fills the night with a ribbon of uncountable pinpoints of light. It humbles you.

"I mean, tomorrow I could be killed by a bear and in the scheme of things, what would it matter," I remark to The Mechanic, who is sitting next to me in the canoe.

"It would mean a lot," he replies. "We'd have to drag your ugly remains outta here. Two days in a canoe with a smelly stiff ain't my idea of fun."

"No, I mean, life on Earth is nothing when you compare it to the millions of worlds out there," I continue.

"Yeah, just a speck on a particle of fly poop," he mutters.

"Awesome isn't it."

"Yeah."

Suddenly I notice one of the stars moving. I watch as it streaks across the curtain of stars.

"Hey look! A satellite," I say as I point at the moving dot of light.

"Probably a spy satellite," The Mechanic says.

"You think so?"

"Yeah, and I bet it's taking pictures of us right now. I hear tell those things can see a football on a field."

"Not much interesting to photograph out here unless you like treetops," I remark.

"Can you imagine some scientist in Russia looking over stuff the satellite has sent back and sees our campfire," The Mechanic says.

"Hey, the Russians I don't mind. Just think if one of those satellites is owned by the Canada Ministry of Natural Resources," I reply.

"Ah, comeon."

"Why not," I continue. "It would be an effective way of keeping tabs on all the fishermen on all these remote lakes. I can just imagine a warden dropping his float plane on the lake above us and paddling down to our camp.

"He'd walk into camp and announce: 'Boys, I'm afraid you're under arrest.' And we'd ask: 'What for?' And he'd say: 'For catching too many of our precious fish.' And we'd say: 'Hey, we obeyed the limits.' We would figure there would be no way he'd know how many fish we'd actually caught.

"Then he would reach into his shoulder pack and pull out a folder of photographs and lay them on the ground. The photographs would show aerial views of the lake we had been fishing the day before. The warden would then pull out more pictures. 'These are blow ups,' he'd explain.

"There on the blow ups would be our canoes," I continue. "Then he'd hand one of us a magnifying lense and tell that person to look at the photographs. And the magnifying lense would reveal not only the canoes, but the fish in the bottoms of the canoes.

"Then the warden would say: 'Count em and weep.'"

The Mechanic gives me a strange look and then turns his attention back to the stars just as a meteor shoots across the sky.

"I hope it hits that blasted satellite. That would show those snooping Ruskies," The Mechanic says with a grin.

"Could be worse," I say.

"How so?"

"Might not be a satellite at all."

"You mean, a UFO?"

"Yeah."

"Are you nuts," The Mechanic says shaking his head.

"Hey, this is the perfect place. I mean, no one ever sees UFOs in crowded places. They always see them in swamps and other remote places," I assert. "If you were bringing a spaceship down on Earth, you'd surely not land in Times Square. No, you'd land in some remote place like this so that you could scope out the situation before encountering any intelligent life."

"What do you mean by that?" The Mechanic asks with a hint of sharpness in his voice.

"I didn't mean you," I assure him. "I'm just saying that a spaceship could land in a place like this and remain undetected. That's how its done on *Star Trek*."

I pause for a moment to look up at the stars.

Then I turn to The Mechanic: "Say, if a flying saucer landed right here and now, and a little green man got out, what would you do?"

The Mechanic thinks for a moment.

"Offer him a beer."

"What?"

"Heck, after traveling across the universe a guy's got to be thirsty"

"Thirsty?"

"Hey can you imagine the little guy going home with a hangover and a passion for cheap beer," The Mechanic laughs.

I look up at the stars and sigh.

CAMPSIDE CHRONICLES

Purchasing a pole is a real pain

"I think it is time I teach you how to fish," I tell my 5-year-old daughter.

She gives me a blank look.

"You are the daughter of a Wildwoods Dad who feels an obligation to pass on his skill and knowledge of the art of fishing," I continue.

She starts to walk away. I grab her arm.

"First thing you'll need is a rod and reel," I say as I pull her toward the car. "We'll just go down to the store and fix you up proper."

She begins to show a little interest. To her and her younger sister, stores are big indoor playgrounds.

"Can you please take the 3-year-old?" my wife asks as I walk out the door.

Before I can say no, she has pushed the child out the door. My wife knows that to deny a 3-year-old a trip in the car would invite a fierce temper tantrum.

Nowadays selecting a rod and reel is a relatively difficult task. It would be nice if stores stocked a dozen or so rods and reels instead of hundreds.

I usually pick a rod based on price— the cheaper the better, figuring that I'll probably break off the tip on the first trip out in the canoe. I have this tendency of setting full packs on my rods or stepping on them while wandering around the campsite after dark.

The instant we walk into the rod and reel department of the store, my daughter spots Mickey Mouse and Sesame Street rod and reel sets. She has no idea what they are. To her, they appear to be fun looking toys.

I look at the price. It is nearly double what a basic rod and reel set sells for.

"How about this one instead?" I ask as I hand her a $5.95 special.

She pays no attention.

"OK, OK. Do you want Mickey Mouse or Sesame Street?"

Without hesitation she picks out the Mickey Mouse set and quickly starts taking apart the package. I take it away from her and put it in the cart.

Suddenly the 3-year-old, who has been peacefully sitting in the cart, comes alive. She grabs the package and starts ripping it open.

The 5-year-old shrieks. "Daddy! She has my Mickey Mouse pole and is ruining it. It's mine. Take it away from her!"

I pull the package away from the little tyke, who instantly takes offense and commences to cry loudly.

I quickly throw the package into the cart, pick up the 3-year-old and carry her down the aisle. "You stay here while I go get some hooks and bobbers." I yell back to the 5-year-old.

The second I disappear around the corner, my eldest daughter has the rod and reel package out of the cart and out of its package. When I return, I find her whipping the rod around like a willow stick.

I put down the 3-year-old and race down the aisle. Meanwhile the 5-year-old discovers the button on the reel which releases the line. As if she inherited the skill, she presses the button at the right moment and actually accomplishes a cast. Normally I would have been filled with fatherly pride. Unfortunately her cast sent the rubber weight attached to the end of the line flying into the backside of an elderly lady's head.

I grab the pole away from my daughter just as the lady turns to see what hit her. Seeing me with the pole, she assumes I hit her and gives me a look that would have made a pro wrestler cower.

"Let's get out of here kids, no fish biting in this section." My eldest daughter gives me another blank look. Suddenly I notice that daughter number two is missing.

"Where's your sister?"

I look down the aisle where I had set her down. She isn't there. I put the 5-year-old in the cart and take off so fast the front wheels lift off the floor.

We race down the aisles and nearly collide with carts pushed by big and burly fishermen.

Then I hear laughter. I stop the cart. You don't often hear laughter in a fishing department. Fishermen are dead serious when it comes to buying tackle. About the only thing you ever hear is a groan when someone looks at the price of a rod or reel they have fallen in love with.

I start moving toward the laughter. I figure if there is anything unusual happening, my 3-year-old is somehow involved.

I turn the corner and abruptly stop. For several moments I stare in disbelief. In the few short minutes she was gone, my little bundle of energy had cleaned off one side of the aisle of every blister pack of tackle she could reach. The small packages are scattered down the aisle as if a sudden wind had torn them off their hooks.

My daughter looks up at me and smiles. Then she picks a bright orange bobber off the floor and whips it at me. Instead of flying toward me, the bobber flies over the display rack into the next aisle and nearly hits a rather scuzzy looking man.

I put the 3-year-old in the seat of the cart and tell her and her sister to stay put. Then I bend down to pick up dozens of Daredevils on the floor.

While I'm playing stock boy, my eldest daughter grabs the fishing pole from the bottom of the cart. Standing up in the cart like some pro angler in a bass boat, she starts casting. I don't discover this until I hear her crying. I look up and discover she has cast her line into a display of spinners. The line has become entangled in the blister packs and display hooks.

As I untangle her line from the display rack and cast nervous glances at the group of people watching me, I begin to wonder if I would be violating the code of the Wildwoods if I passed onto my daughters something other than a love of fishing.

A night of air mattress madness

"This is luxury," I told my wife as I took the doubled-size air mattress out of the box.

"Anything is better than the ground," she remarked and walked away.

"I wish I had had one of these things along for the Canada's Curse canoe trip," I said to myself.

On the canoe trip all I allow myself is one of those roll up, self-inflating mattresses. It's all that one can carry. To lug a full-size air mattress along would be inviting a hernia, or worse, some snide comments from the rest of the crew.

Oh, the roll up mattress does provide somewhat of a buffer between the rock hard ground and your body. But it isn't what I'd call comfortable. For one thing, I tend to slide off the mattress in the middle of the night. I also feel every rock and root in the ground.

Getting a good night's sleep is a real challenge when you are roughing it. I find a couple of good, stiff belts of whiskey help get me through the initial discomfort.

But an air mattress is something else. An air mattress puts a six-inch layer of air between you and whatever is on the ground. You could sleep on a rock field and feel like you were sleeping on a bed of soft moss.

"I'll just blow it up and we'll be all set," I said to my wife as I spread the deflated mattress across the ground. "I'll just use the portable tire pump in the car."

I plugged the portable tire pump into the cigarette lighter and carried it over to the mattress. I turned the mattress around until I found the valve.

But it wasn't a valve.

It was a tube.

A big tube.

No way would the end of the portable tire pump work with a tube.

"What are we going to do?" My wife asked nervously.

"Well, I'll just blow it up like a balloon," I said as I wrapped my lips around the end of the tube. I took a deep breath and blew. I heard air go into the mattress, but I didn't see any signs of inflation. "Hey, I've blown up many air mattresses before at the beach. This is no different."

My wife glanced at the mattress and then me. "I think this is significantly bigger than a beach air mattress."

"So it takes me a few minutes longer," I said between puffs. I felt the world spinning.

After three minutes of puffing, I noticed only one small

71

corner of the air mattress had risen. The rest was as flat as an empty garbage bag.

"I don't think I've got the lung power for this," I said as I capped the fill tube.

Just then a young couple who had been walking down the road came up to me.

"You'll never blow that sucker up," the man told me. "You need one of those oversized foot pumps."

"Great, why didn't they tell me that when I bought it," I said angrily.

"They did, dear," my wife interrupted. "Remember the clerk asked if you wanted the pump and you said you wouldn't need it because you already had a pump."

"I meant my portable tire pump!"

"He didn't know that."

"So what do I do?" I asked as I looked down at the flat mattress.

"Well, you could use a hair dryer," the young man suggested.

"A hair dryer?"

"Sure, I've heard it works quite well providing you put it on the coolest setting. Otherwise you'll melt your mattress. Then you just press the end against the fill tube and turn it on. They say it works like a charm."

"Great! Do you have a hair dryer?" I asked my wife.

"Yeah, sure. Comeon if I would have packed a hair dryer, you would have screamed. You would have told me 'Now what would you do with a hairdryer at a campsite without power!'"

I looked up at the young couple.

"Sorry, we don't have one, either," the woman said.

As the young couple walked off, I sat staring at the mattress. Then an idea hit.

"Maybe the park ranger has one!" I shouted.

"Hey, I'm not going up to a man I don't know and ask him if he has a hair dryer," my wife said shaking her head.

"Oh, I'll go," I replied as I gathered up the mattress in my arms and threw it into the back of the van.

"Don't you think it is a little late," my wife said.

I looked at my watch: 9:00 p.m. "He'll understand."

Five minutes later I pulled up to the park station and went inside. The park ranger was just getting ready to make his rounds through the campground.

"Do you have a hair dryer?" I asked.

"Say what?"

"A hair dryer."

He gave me a strange look and then continued fiddling with the flashlight in his hands. "Needs new batteries," he mumbled to himself.

"I need a hair dryer," I said a little more forcefully.

"Gee, don't get many requests for hair dryers. Firewood, yes, but hair dryers? I think most people can get by with a towel. I mean, you don't need a blow dry look out here."

"Oh, no, it isn't for me, it is for my air mattress," I said with a smile.

"You're going to blow dry your mattress?" he asked with a puzzled look.

"No, I need the hair dryer to blow it up," I said.

"Never heard of anyone doing that before. Most people have these big foot pumps," he replied.

"Do you have one of those?"

"Nope."

"Know where I can find one?"

"Not at this time of night."

"How about a hair dryer?"

"Afraid not," the ranger said apologetically. After he thought a minute, he added, "Why not try the gas station in town."

"That's 10 miles from here!"

"Afraid that's your only option."

I thanked him for his time and returned to my car. It was close to 9:30 p.m. As he said, I didn't have much choice. I started the van and headed toward town. Fifteen minutes later I pulled into a gas station.

"Got a hair dryer?" I asked the rather burly attendant.

He gave me one of those give-me-a-break-you-dumb-city-slicker looks.

"I need it for my air mattress," I explained as I pointed to the deflated pile of plastic I had dragged in.

"Don't have a hair dryer, but you can use the air hose over there," he said.

"Thanks," I said as I walked over to the air hose. I stuck the end of the hose into the fill tube and squeezed the lever to release the air. Nothing happened. I squeezed again. Nothing.

"Ya have to press in the stem," the attendant said after watching me struggle for a minute or two.

"What stem?"

"The stem inside the valve," he said pointing to the brass fitting at the end of the air hose. He pressed it in while holding down the lever and the air hose let loose with a mighty hiss.

I took the hose from him, put my thumbnail on the stem and held it in the fill tube of the air mattress which I held in my other hand. With both hands occupied, I couldn't press down the air hose lever.

"Could you help me?" I asked the attendant.

He smiled one of those boy-the-people-you-meet-during-the-tourist-season smiles and bent down to squeeze the lever.

Hissssssss.

Ten seconds later the mattress was fully inflated.

"Boy, does that work slick!" I exclaimed as I quickly capped the mattress's fill tube.

The attendant didn't seem as impressed and walked away mumbling to himself.

"Now I'll just get this into the van," I said as I opened the back door. I picked up the feather-light mattress and aimed one end at the open door.

It wouldn't go in.

74

The mattress was about eight inches bigger than the opening of the door.

I put the mattress on an angle.

It still wouldn't go.

It was now 10:15 p.m.

I grabbed some rope from the backseat and then threw the mattress up on the luggage rack. I carefully crisscrossed the mattress with the rope. I got into the van, waved to the attendant and drove off.

Two miles down the road, my eyes caught something in the rearview mirror. It was the air mattress bouncing down the highway like a huge basketball.

I slammed on the brakes, pulled the van to the side of the road and took off running for the fleeing mattress.

A stiff westerly wind kept the mattress moving briskly, but I was gaining on it. I was just within a few yards of it when I saw headlights.

"Omigosh!" I screamed as I dove for the ditch.

I watched helplessly as a semi slammed into the air mattress. The mattress exploded into hundreds of pieces—some clung to the truck, others flew up into the air like leaves in a breeze. The truck never stopped.

It was 11:00 p.m. by the time I got back to the campsite.

My wife was already asleep in her sleeping bag on top of the roll up, self-inflating mattress I take up to Canada.

I held up a piece of plastic no bigger than a potholder, sighed and then crawled into my own sleeping bag which rested on the cold and awfully uncomfortable ground.

Welcome to spider city

I don't want to alarm you, but have you ever looked underneath the picnic tables at a state park campsite?

If you are the kind of person who likes to read Stephen King novels at bedtime, you might enjoy the thrill of looking underneath these seemingly innocent tables.

But if you are a person who can barely tolerate the creatures which inhabit campsites, then I suggest that under no circumstances, short of dropping a $10 bill, you venture underneath a campsite table.

It wasn't until a recent visit to a state park that I discovered the horror beneath the boards...

We were enjoying a feast of lukewarm hotdogs, soggy buns and overcooked baked beans, when all of a sudden my 5-year-old shrieked and jumped off her seat.

"Spider, daddy, a spider!"

Sure enough, walking across her plate was a rather healthy looking daddy longlegs. I resisted my family's urgings that I kill the beast. I didn't have the stomach to squash a spider and pick its remains from a plate of baked beans.

Moments later the spider walked off the plate, continued across the table and disappeared off the edge.

I looked on the ground. He was nowhere to be seen. Where did he go? For some odd reason, I found myself bound and determined to discover where that peripatetic spider went off to.

I lowered my head so that I could see underneath the tabletop.

"AAAARGH!"

"What is it dear?" my wife asked.

I couldn't answer. I had to catch my breath first.

"Let me see," my 5-year-old said excitedly.

"No!" I yelled. "If you value your sleep at night, don't look under there."

"Why not?" my wife asked.

"It's too horrible."

"You mean the spider?"

"Spiders, dear, spiders! It's an alien world inhabited by monsters."

"You're exaggerating."

"I tell you there are millions of them under there, a regular New York City of spiders. There are big ones, little ones, sleeping ones, moving ones all woven together in one huge mass of interconnecting web."

My wife got up from her seat and moved away from the table. The 3-year-old stayed at the table oblivious to her parents' concern. The 5-year-old made another try at looking under the table, but mother's hand was too quick.

"Well, what are you going to do about it?" my wife asked.

"Uh, nothing, I guess." I replied weakly. "I mean, they do have a right to be there. They were living under that table long before we got here. I suspect we could move."

"Let's."

"Before we do, let me just check out a few other tables in the campgrounds. Maybe they are all like that," I suggested and went walking down the road.

I wandered into a campsite and greeted a young couple sitting in lawn chairs and reading newspapers.

"Hi," I said cheerfully. " Mind if I look under your picnic table."

They gave me a rather odd look, a look which said— Hey, we left the city to get away from people like you. Reluctantly they nodded their heads.

"Looking for anything in particular?" the man asked nervously.

"Uh, no," I replied evasively.

The couple looked at each other, shrugged their shoulders and went back to reading their newspapers.

Suddenly I let out with an unintentional gasp. The couple

looked up from their papers.

"Anything wrong?" the woman asked.

"Uh, no," I said quickly as I tried to resume normal breathing.

"Are you sure? You look a little pale," she continued.

"Uh, I'm fine. I gotta go now." I quickly left the campsite.

Unfortunately I must have left them curious, because an hour later I noticed they and all their camping gear were gone.

We stayed. My wife, in a rather surprising show of courage and strength, had gone to an adjacent campsite and had asked to borrow a broom. She then swept our problem back into the woods. I told her I didn't think that was a wise idea.

"Now we'll have a bunch of displaced spiders running around. They may seek revenge for their abrupt relocation."

"Donald, I don't want to hear about it," my wife said sharply.

"They could come looking for us tonight..."

"DONALD!"

"All right. But when we get back home, I'm writing a letter to Stephen King. This would make a heck of a story...."

"I don't want to hear about it."

"I can just see the movie. A bunch of teenagers decide to spend a weekend at... uh... Spider Lake campground. And one of the boys kills a spider for no apparent reason. It turns out to be the king spider..."

"Donald, I'm taking the kids to the beach."

"OK, I'll go with you."

"No you won't"

"Why not?"

"Because you'll start telling that spider story..."

"Movie dear, movie. We'll be rich. You see, after the kid kills the spider, the other spiders seek revenge and one by one the teenagers mysteriously perish until there are just two left. You know, the innocent blonde with the heart of gold and the pimple faced boy who loves her, but can't find a way to express it because

78

he thinks, she thinks, he's a nerd, which he is, at least on the outside, but inside he's a hero..."

"Run that by me again," my wife said as she shook her head.

"Don't worry about the details, dear. Anyway, the movie rises to a thrilling conclusion as these two young kids rely on inner resources they never realized they had, to do battle with billions of spiders charging out from everywhere..."

"Oh, give me a break!" My wife groaned as she gathered up the beach towels and headed toward the car with the kids.

"I tell you we're going to make millions, my little spiders and me." I said as I glanced over at the picnic table and watched a daddy longlegs walk across the tabletop.

Campstove causes conniption fits

Someday someone is going to design a foolproof campstove. But I doubt it will happen in my lifetime.

It's amazing the difference between what campstove manufacturers claim and how the darn things actually perform.

"We took our DDX-1 Super Propane Cookstove to the Antarctic and it fired up first time, every time," the ad said.

Well, every campstove I've ever taken along on a canoe trip works fine so long as the sun is shining.

But try to light it in a pouring rain or after sundown when it's freezing outside. I guarantee the thing won't light on the first try, or the second or the third.

On several occasions, I have sat watching my little backpack stove cook itself after the whole thing has exploded into flame. It's one reason I always wear a big hat. Works great for stove fires.

One time I got so mad at the darn thing, I put on a pair of

leather gloves, picked up the flaming thing and whipped it like a softball. It flew through the night sky like a fireball before crashing into a pine tree. The impact put out the flame and for some odd reason, the darn thing has worked great ever since.

Even in less rugged conditions, cookstoves are finicky, as the following story illustrates...

It's 8:30 p.m. and it is getting dark. We've been driving all day to get to this campground.

The kids are starving. For the past hour, my wife has defended a bag of cookies against full-scale assaults by the kids.

After we reach the campsite, I pull the three burner cookstove out of the back of the van and quickly set it up on the picnic table. As my wife holds a flashlight, I connect the hose from the propane cannister to the stove.

Slowly I turn on one of the burners and strike a match.

Nothing happens.

I turn the burner knob again, this time listening for that distinctive hiss.

I hear nothing.

I smell nothing.

The match burns down and singes the tips of my fingers.

My wife turns off the flashlight as I let loose with a series of not-so-nice words.

"Ssshhhh! The kids will hear you," she scolds.

"Heck, the girls aren't paying attention. They are too busy looking for the cookies you hid. By the way, where did you hide them?

"In your sleeping bag," she says quietly.

"Point the light over here." I unscrew the hose and look at the threads—I have no idea what I'm looking for—and then screw the hose back on, this time giving it a few hard turns.

I turn on the burner.

Nothing.

I unscrew the end of the hose going into the stove, take a look at the threads and then screw it back in.

80

I turn on the burner.

Hissssssssss.

"Got a match?"

"No," my wife replies flatly.

I quickly pat the pockets of my shirt and pants. Nothing.

"Shine the light around."

My wife moves the flashlight in a broad sweep. About 10 feet from the picnic table is my butane lighter. I turn off the burner and go to pick up the lighter. I return and turn the burner back on.

Nothing.

"Maybe we should go into town," my wife suggests. "Swearing at a stove isn't putting food on the table."

I slam my fist against the side of the cookstove and turn the burner knob.

Hisssssssss.

I quickly flick the lighter.

WHOOOOSH

YEEEEEEEHOOOOOOUCH

The burner is on; the hair is off the back of my hand.

I grab a pan, throw a can of soup into it and place it on the stove.

"Dinner will be served in 10 minutes," I announce.

As I go to look for the buns , my eldest girl wanders over to the cookstove and watches the flames lick the bottom of the pan. Then for some reason known only to her, she reaches up and turns the burner off.

"HEY, get a way from there!" I yell.

She backs off.

I walk over, turn on the burner and flick my lighter.

The lighter ignites, but the stove doesn't.

We eventually sit down to a supper of lukewarm soup and peanut butter and jelly sandwiches.

An hour later, I'm getting ready for bed.

Exhausted by my ordeal with the cookstove, frustrated by a less than smooth start to a weekend camping trip, and sore from the first degree burns on my hand, I decide to hit the sack early.

I crawl into my tent, unroll my sleeping bag and slide in.

CRUNCH.

"What's that?" I ask my wife.

"I think you just went to bed in tomorrow's dessert," she sighs and rolls over.

Computer assisted camp planning

I'm a computer assisted camper, a modern technological woodland wonder.

Recently I have been using my home computer to plan and prepare for family camping outings. I must say it has made things a lot easier.

One of the hardest aspects of camping for the Oakland family has been forgetting to take things, minor things like tents, sleeping bags and food supplies. Here's the story of how I used a computer to attempt to solve the problem...

"I thought you packed it," my wife says indignantly.

"I told you to," I reply as I frantically search for the camp cook kit.

"No you didn't"

"Yes I did."

In an effort to avoid such counterproductive camping, my wife and I have resorted to making sophisticated and comprehensive lists.

A weekend trip to the northwoods usually means the preparing of a three or four page list.

It's a real pain to write everything down, check everything

off at least two times and constantly add or subtract things from the master list.

But that was before the computer era hit the Oakland household. Now things run so effortlessly...

"Do you think we should pack the old or new toothbrushes for the kids," I yell to my wife as I enter outdoor items into my PC in the basement.

"What? I can't hear you. You'll have to come upstairs," My wife shouts back.

I leave my basement office and head for the bedroom. There my wife is ankle deep in clothes, some piled so high on the bed they resemble a Rocky Mountain range.

"Dear, what toothbrushes should we pack for the kids?"

"Oh, I don't care," she says sharply.

"Is something wrong?"

"Donald, you have been in that basement for two hours. When are you going to come up here and help me pack?"

"I will in a moment. I've just got to enter the last twenty items into my database."

"Donald, forget the database. Just print out a list of what we have to take and then come up here and help me pack," she says as she pushes a wad of clothing into an overly stuffed backpack.

"Print out a list? Dear this is no ordinary Boy-Scout-Be-Prepared camping list. This is a sophisticated, cross indexed, multi-layered database. For example, I can sort out everything by who needs what. Why, I can tell you how many pair of underwear we should pack for each girl..."

"Donald, I know how many pair we packed because I was packing them while my husband was hiding in the basement with his blasted computer."

"Dear, join the 20th century. Why I'll be able..." Suddenly I'm struck by a grand inspiration. "If I assign square inches to each item of our camping trip....and put them in a computed field...why I'll be able to predict how much space our camping gear will take up in the van!"

83

"Donald, who cares...we always manage to stuff everything in the van," my wife says as she trips over a toy car hidden under a T-shirt.

"Honey, unpack all that stuff. I'll get a ruler and a calculator..."

"Over my dead body!" she shrieks

"OK, OK, I'll estimate this time."

I quickly leave the bedroom and return to my basement office to enter more valuable data into my mini mainframe.

"Let's see, a T-shirt is roughly 18 inches by 12 inches..." I mumble to myself. "Nah, that's not right because a T-shirt will be folded...let's see, folded twice it would be 6 inches wide, 3 inches long and 5 inches deep..."

It is well after midnight before I complete my camping database. It is now time to pop open a beer and watch as the computer spits out page after page of data.

After the printout is complete, I scoop it and rush upstairs to share this technological triumph with my wife.

"Well, let's start packing dear, the list is complete. All we have to do is just check off when we pack..."

I stop when I realize my wife is asleep, her head resting on a bulging backpack and her body covered with an unrolled sleeping bag. Around her is all our gear, neatly packed.

I lift her into bed, return to the livingroom for another beer and another look at my marvelous camping database.

"Boy, computers certainly make preparing for a camping trip a lot easier," I tell myself.

Rambo I ain't

I get really upset when I watch a Rambo or Crocodile Dundee movie.

When you see them up there on the big screen, what do they always have?

A knife...a big knife...a humongous knife.

Even in the love scenes, they always have their big blade at their side.

Why couldn't they just carry a pocketknife?

Someday one of my daughters will see a Rambo or Croc D. movie and during a subsequent camping trip she will come up to me and ask why I don't carry a big knife like those guys do. Instantly daddy's manhood will be threatened. I mean, when we go camping or fishing, about the biggest thing I ever carry is my ever-handy Swiss Army knife.

When the question arises, I will take my daughter aside, pull out my little ol' jackknife, start whittling on a small stick and say something like this...

"Darling, Rambo carries a big knife because he needs it to annihilate armies. I mean, you can't wipe out a battalion of Ruskies with a 3-inch blade, can opener and nail clipper.

"On the other hand, Mr. Dundee carries a big knife to kill crocodiles. To the best of my knowledge, there isn't a crocodile within 5,000 miles of here, except in a zoo or two. Should I ever meet up with a crocodile, it is unlikely I'd go after him with a knife, no matter how big a blade it has. A Howitzer would be my weapon of choice.

"Anyway, neither Mr. Rambo nor Mr. Dundee have to lug their big knives any farther than on and off a movie set. Your daddy can barely handle a backpack. Put a two pound hunk of steel on his belt and he'd collapse on the spot.

"I may not be as macho as Rambo, but I'm a heckuva lot smarter having this Swiss Army knife," I tell her as the blade of my knife slips off the stick and buries itself into my thumb.

What I wouldn't tell her is I do indeed have a Crocodile Dundee knife. I acquired it while I was in college.

A friend and I got it in our heads we'd like to try the sport of knife throwing. Somewhere we found an ad for a catalog of throwing knives and a $5.95 "how-to book."

I ended up ordering something called an Ax-knife, 16 ounces of pure high-tempered steel. It was darn near two-foot long and so heavy that when I put it on my belt I had a hard time keeping my pants up.

After classes, my friend and I would find a big, dead tree somewhere and throw knives at it. It was great fun, particularly when the knives would actually stick in the wood, which occurred once out of every five throws.

Our knife throwing came to an abrupt halt one day when the knife I had thrown missed its mark, glanced off the side of the tree trunk, flew 20 yards and slammed into the side of my friend's 1970 Mercury Cougar.

To this day, I have never seen an odder look on a man than the look that body shop manager gave us when he saw that knife. The entire length of its blade was embedded perfectly perpendicular in the car door.

I still have the knife. It's rusting in some dark recess of my basement.

Someday I'll get it out, strap it onto my belt, take off my shirt, put on my Adventureland hat from Disneyland, and show my daughters that their daddy can be Crocodile Dundee, too.

My only worry is whether my wife's heart could withstand all the laughing.

Spider causes terror in the tent

You are never alone in the woods.

Even bundled up in your sleeping bag inside your tent with all hundred and one zippers tightly fastened, you have company.

"Daddy!"

"What," I grumbled as I lifted my head out of my sleeping bag, looked over my wife's bag and saw my eldest daughter standing on her bag.

"There's a spider in the tent, it's a big spider...I'm scared."

I groped for my glasses which I found slightly bent underneath my sleeping bag and put them on. To my surprise, I couldn't see a thing. The humidity inside the tent had frosted the lenses with a heavy dew. I wiped them on the sleeves of my pajamas and put my glasses back on.

"Where's the flashlight?" I said as my hand danced around amongst the clutter on either side of the sleeping bag.

"I've got it," my daughter said.

"Darling, don't take daddy's flashlight...

"But I had to go potty."

"Daddy needs the flashlight if he is to protect his family or see what time it is... 2 a.m.! It's 2 in the morning, go back to bed!"

"But daddy there's a spider, I'm scared."

"A spider won't hurt you...A bear might, but a spider... no way.

"Bear!??"

"Forget I said that."

"But daddy what if he crawls in my nose!"

"A spider has more sense than to crawl into someone's nose."

"Daddy kill it, please, or I'll have bad dreams."

"OK, OK," I said realizing there was no way I was going to

convince my daughter of the relative harmlessness of spiders. I also realized that if our conversation would continue we would awaken my wife– a fate worse than any encounter with a spider– or awaken the 3-year-old– who would scream loud enough to awaken the entire campground.

"Where is it?"

"Up there," she replied pointing at the center point of the tent's roof.

I crawled out of my bag, got onto my knees and looked up. "Omigosh! That's no spider...It's a monster!" I yelled.

The spider was as big as my fist. It was a huge black bugger dangling from a strand of web as thick as clothesline. The shock of seeing such a massive arachnid caused me to lose my balance and fall across my wife like a tall maple felled by a lumberjack.

In her half awakened state, my wife apparently thought she was being attacked by a bear and began hitting me with both fists as she screamed wildly.

"It's me, IT'S ME"

"Donald, what are you doing?"

"Quiet dear, there's a monster spider in the tent."

"Where?"

"There."

"Big deal."

"Big deal! Dear the thing is as big as a baseball with legs like an octopus."

"That little thing," she said with a voice sounding half confused, half disgusted.

I flicked on the flashlight and pointed it upward. Instead of the awesome crawler I had seen just minutes before, there was a miniscule daddy longlegs. "Dear, I've never seen anything like it...a shrinking spider."

"Donald, turn off the light."

"What?"

"Turn off the flashlight for a moment," my wife said calmly.

"Daddy, the spider will get us," my daughter said as she

quickly crawled inside her sleeping bag.

I turned off the light and suddenly the spider grew 10 times as big and leaped halfway across the top of the tent. It was at that moment I realized that what I had first seen was not a spider at all, but the shadow of a daddy longlegs bathing in the light of a full moon filtering through the sheer fabric of the tent's roof.

I stood up, aimed the flashlight at the tiny insect. With two fingers I plucked the spider from the side of the tent and gently carried it to the back door, opened the zipper and flung the beast to a new homeland.

"There can we go back to sleep now?'

I turned the light on my daughter who was fast asleep and on my wife who was wide awake.

Suddenly the 3-year-old awakened and started screaming and she didn't stop for the next 20 minutes.

Fish not biting?
All you need
is a little motivation

The other day I had a marvelous idea for making millions... Motivational tapes for fishermen.

I got the idea while doing dishes.

Of late I have been listening to motivational tapes while doing the dishes. It's great. Listening to these guys really gets me enthused and I find I tend to do the dishes faster. And I have a better attitude toward dish washing.

You know the kind of tapes I'm talking about. For $500 the guy doing the tape will come to your town and with all the passion of a Southern Baptist preacher, he'll tell you how life is great and how your life is great and how it is getting better and better every day...

Then he'll say something like...

"Considering the alternative, be thankful you woke up this morning. What a great way to start the day: Awake, alive and filled with the potential to make it big."

Heck, I think I could be a pretty good motivational speaker. All I'd have to do is develop a Southern accent. I don't know why, but it seems like every motivational speaker I have ever heard has a bit of drawl mixed in with all that inspiration.

Since there seems to be a fair number of motivational speakers for business, sports, schools and women's clubs, I figure to find my niche in fishing.

So sit back and let me make you feel good about fishing...

Fish not biting...

Aren't catching 'em when they do...

Boat motor never works right...

Can't seem to pull a muskie from that weedbed you've been fishing since you were six...

Don't despair.

It's your attitude, my friend.

There's a lot of negativism in that boat with you. Yes sir, Mr. Negativism has got you in his net.

Let me tell you a little story... When I was growing up near Lake Wunderful, I used to catch fish by the dozen. Wasn't a day that I didn't get my limit of bass, northern, perch... you name it I've caught it.

But the older I got the less fish I caught. I was using the same bait, the same lures, but catching less fish. And those I did catch were smaller.

I was hurtin'.

I read every fishing book I could. Went to every sports show around. I bought the newest rods and reels and filled five tackle boxes with lures.

Nothing worked.

Then one day I was fishing on the Golijee River when my boat drifted by an old man in an ancient, paint-peeled johnboat. I wouldn't have paid much attention to the old man, 'cept he had one heckuva stringer of fish. Biggest bass I'd ever seen.

Well, I dropped anchor next to him and asked him what his secret was. He looked at me, smiled and said one word—Attitude.

Attitude?

He said "Boy, look to the west. What do you see?" I told him I saw a sunset. "Is that all?" I nodded. Then he said, "I see beauty; I see the end of a marvelous day, a day that was such a privilege to have experienced..." As he talked, he pulled in a 42-inch northern which he then let go. "I feel its energy and its goodness." He threw out his line again and moments later reeled in a big bellied bass.

"Attitude. Fish can smell it. Your best lure is your self image, my friend," he told me as he let the bass go.

That old man was filled with joy and life. Every time he cast, he cast out love and enthusiasm for life. Why the spoon on the end of his line shone with PMA... positive mental attitude.

A lot of you feel guilty when you get into that boat. Oh, you won't admit it, but you feel it. You should be home doing chores. You shouldn't have spent the kid's lunch money on that new lure. You shouldn't have mortgaged your house and your family's future for a $15,995 bass boat.

Get rid of the guilt.

You deserve that time in your boat. You've earned it with all your hard work and all your responsibilities. This is your time! This is your place!

Take a deep breath of the morning air and hold it. Smell the woods and shores. Listen to the waves. Feel the strength of nature pouring into your body.

You know, man is too darn distracted to feel nature's strength. Other animals feel it. Ever seen an unhappy deer? Shake that guilt, feel the power, my friends.

Repeat after me...

91

I feel good, things are great and getting better and better in every way every day.

I feel strong; I feel nature; I feel like fishing today.

And keep saying that to yourself as you put your boat into the water, as you tug on that starter rope and as you open that tackle box.

You'll find you'll cast farther.

Fish finder! Throw it away. You are in tune with yourself and with nature and that, my friend, is the best fish finder in the whole wide wonderfully wet world of ours.

You're not out there to catch fish; you are out there to rejoice in nature and re-energize those self concept batteries. Live for the experience.

If you're positive, the perch will bite.

If you believe, the bass will be there.

If you cast with love, you'll reel in lunkers.

Now I want you to grab your pole, pick up that tacklebox and walk out of here with your head high and proud to fish!

Techno-camping is coming

Computers have found their way into darn near every aspect of our lives.

And I can envision the day when computers will accompany us camping...

We pull into Crystal Lake Campgrounds near Woodruff, Wisconsin. It is a bright, sunny Friday morning.

"Are you sure they'll have a site open?" my wife asks with a hint of worry.

"No problem. Just before coming I plugged my Apple computer into CampSat, a telephone campsite reservation network. I called up Crystal Lake on my computer and the network indicated there were six campsites currently available, 15 that would be available tomorrow and 20 that would be open the following day. Half of those sites are next to the lake."

"Did you make a reservation?"

"Sure did, I entered my VISA number and within moments got back on my printer confirmation that we had a campsite on the southside of the lake."

"That's nice dear," she replies, her voice now more relaxed.

I walk into the ranger's station. Behind the counter is a young girl in a khaki uniform. She is seated at a computer terminal and busily entering information she is receiving over her telephone headset.

"Thank you Mr. Froelich, your campsite reservation is confirmed," the girl tells the caller and then turns to us.

"Can I help you?"

"The name's Oakland. We have a reservation for a campsite for today and tomorrow."

The girl turns to her computer monitor, quickly strikes a few keys and then grimaces.

"I don't have anything for Oakland."

"You must, I just entered it this morning."

"Did you punch in your VISA number?"

"Yes."

"Your name?"

"Yup."

"Your 10-digit CampSat identification number and DNR billing code."

"Uh?"

"Sir?"

"Yeah, I did," I reply as I rip through my wallet looking for my personalized CampSat card. "Yeah, I entered 4489103266, or at least I think I did."

I glance at the confirmation print out. I study the numbers in the upper right hand corner 4...489...1032...65...What? 65. "Uh, oh! I think I missed one number. Could you check 4489103265?" I ask the girl.

"Yes I have a reservation for that number, a very nice campsite with a southern view of the lake."

"That's ours," I say with relief.

"No it isn't"

"What do you mean?"

"That campsite is reserved by a Mr. D.B. Donnelly of Lodi, Wisconsin."

"Ma'am, Mr. Donnelly has no intention of camping this weekend, he is merely a typographical error. You can see that?"

"I suspect you're right."

"Well, change it."

"I can't."

"You can't?"

"Even if I wanted to, there is no way I can override the Campsat files."

"Okay, just pretend I'm Mr. Donnelly?"

The girl sighs.

"Mr. Oakland I can't do that either. If I take your VISA number and enter it into the computer as confirmation of payment, the computer will automatically recognize the discrepancy between who is camping and who is paying. It will refuse to enter the transaction."

"I'll pay cash."

"I can't accept cash payment."

I turn to my wife and shrug my shoulders.

"Do something dear, the kids are tearing up the place," she says as she glances at our 3-year-old who has pulled every brochure out of a rack in the corner of the room.

"Okay, what do you have available?"

The girl turns back to her computer and quickly punches a dozen or so keys.

"Crystal Lake is filled. So is Firefly. Now we have a couple sites open on Muskie."

"We'll take one."

"Just a minute," my wife interrupts.

"What dear?"

"I just don't want any old campsite. Tell me what they're like," she says turning to the girl.

The girl punches a few more keys.

"Let's see... Number 12a is in a non-smoking section, has 12 surrounding trees, three of which are mature white pines, a table manufactured in 1976, a fire ring with four logs and a flat area suitable for two tents..."

"That's all well and good, but I just want to know one thing," my wife says somewhat impatiently. "How far is it from the beach and from the toilets."

The girl scrolls through the information on the screen.

"It's 405.6 yards from the beach and 120 yards from the nearest toilet."

"In what direction from the toilet?" my wife asks.

"West."

"Dear!" I interrupt. "Why is that important?"

"I don't want a campsite downwind from a pit toilet."

"We'll take it," I tell the girl.

"Donald!"

"Let me show you something."

I leave the ranger's station and return a few minutes later with a portable computer tucked under my arm. I put it on the counter, open it up and slip in a floppy disk.

"Campers Guide?" The girl says with a hint of admiration in her voice.

"Yup. Version 2a."

"Wow."

I boot the program and enter the word "Wisconsin." The computer asks me longitude and latitude. I enter the numbers and the computer starts humming and clicking.

Seconds later a menu of information appears on the screen. I select "Woodruff." Another chart of data appears. I select "Crystal Lake." The computer hums and clicks.

"You see dear, the prevailing winds are from the north, so the pit toilet odor shouldn't be a problem...Now lets see..." I hit a few keys and a map of the Crystal Lake campgrounds appears.

"What was that number?"

"Number 12a," the girl says.

I punch in Number 12a. A tiny light flashes to indicate the location of the campsite on the map.

I turn to the young girl and lean toward her.

"If you'd let me use your phone, I could plug it into my modem and call CampWeather for the latest one day, weekend and 5-day forecasts."

The girl's eyes widen. She is definitely impressed. I'm just about to make this girl's day when my wife grabs the back of my collar and pulls me out of there.

"Dear, I was just going to broaden that girl's knowledge of outdoor computer technology."

"Sure you were."

Dad experiences tent trauma

"We need a new tent," my wife said as she paged through a mailer from a discount store.

"Terrific," I moaned. "I just spent a small fortune on coolers, lanterns, sleeping bags for the kids and plastic tarps. Can't we wait until next year to buy a tent?"

"I refuse to spent one more night in a two-man tent with two small kids and a husband who snores," she said sternly.

"I don't snore," I protested.

"Look, your tent was real cozy when it was just you and me. It was snug when it was just you and me and one daughter. We now have two children. Trying to put our family in that tent would be like trying to fit the Milwaukee Bucks in a Volkswagen Beetle."

"It wouldn't be that bad," I said.

"Remember the last time we had the two girls in bed with us. The 3-year-old thrashed around so much you woke up to find a foot in your face."

I winced as I remembered that sleepless night. She had me. If four in a tent would be anything like four in a bed, a larger tent would be well worth the money.

"OK, tomorrow we'll go look at tents."

As a kid, I never had anything bigger than a glorified pup tent. The two-man A frame which I now take up to Canada each year is luxurious compared to what I had when I was a Boy Scout. I mention this as an explanation why I suffered from culture shock when I first viewed a "family tent."

"Hey, I want something for camping, not to play sheik of the desert," I said as I walked up to a 9 by 12 foot cabin tent.

"I bet this would be a bear to put up," I said shaking one of the aluminum supports.

"Not at all," a voice replied. I turned around and there was a clerk dressed in a faded gray wool sweater, jeans and Gore-Tex hiking boots—your typical Yuppie camper.

"Actually this model goes up in 10 minutes..."

"Sure if you had a crane and a crew of 10. You've got to understand I have a wife who can't put a two piece pool cue together and two kids who as yet don't fathom the concept of helping dad."

My wife gave me a nasty glance.

"Well it's true, you aren't the most mechanically minded person around."

"Donald! I was a Girl Scout. I'm a college educated woman. I can figure out how to set up a tent," she said glaring at me.

The clerk smiled nervously and quickly stepped inside the tent.

"As you can see there is plenty of room in here," the clerk said with a sweep of his hand.

"I'll say, you could fit a cub scout pack in here."

"Actually, this is just right for a family your size," the clerk continued. "You might think it looks big, but when you are out in the woods and it has been raining all day and shows no sign of letting up, you'll appreciate the room."

"You have a point," I conceded and turned to my wife. "By the way, where are the kids?"

"They were right outside the door," she said poking her head outside the tent. The two girls were nowhere to be seen.

"That's all right," the clerk remarked. "There isn't too much trouble they can get into around here..."

Suddenly we heard a woman scream. The three of us ran out of the tent just in time to see a middle-aged, rather heavyset woman emerge from a large dome tent. She looked shaken and out of breath.

"Are you all right, lady?" the clerk said running up to her.

She glared up at the young man, turned and stomped back into the tent. Moments later she walked out pulling by the arm my 5-year-old, who was wearing nothing but her underwear.

"Whose child is this?" she said indignantly.

"Mine," I replied meekly as my daughter broke from the woman's grip and ran to me.

"Your daughter nearly scared me to death," the woman said as she tried to catch her breath. "I walked into the tent and found two unraveled sleeping bags on the floor. When I bent over to examine them more closely, one flew open and out popped this screaming, half-naked child!"

"We were playing camping, daddy," my daughter explained innocently.

"Where's your sister?"

She pointed to the other bag. I entered the tent and unzipped the bag. Nothing. I glared up at the 5-year-old.

"She was there a minute ago," she replied with a shrug of her shoulders.

Suddenly the sporting goods shop became a huge shell

game— under which tent was the 3-year-old?

I went left; the clerk went right.

She wasn't in the four-man dome tent.

Nor was she hiding in the 8 x 10 cabin tent.

EUREKA! The clerk shouted.

"You found her?" I yelled back.

"Nah, Charlie up front wanted to know the make of a tent I sold this morning." The clerk paused for a moment and then pointed toward the front of the store. "Say what are all those people looking at?"

I turned and noticed about a dozen people standing outside the front door. They were laughing and pointing and waving at something in the front window. Then I noticed my 5-year-old was standing with them. She waved to me.

"I found her dad!" she hollered.

My wife and I ran to front of the store only to discover the 3-year-old had somehow crawled into the display window and had managed to drag one of the mannequins into a small red dome tent. When I reached her, she was trying to stuff the left leg of the mannequin into a sleeping bag.

I scooped up the child, apologized to the clerks and rushed out of the store with my wife and two kids in tow. "I think I'll mail order the new tent," I said to my wife as we got into the car.

I never thought looking for a tent could be so traumatic.

RVs and CDs aren't camping gear

"Daddy, why don't we have one of those?" my eldest daughter asked as she pointed at a large motorhome parked in an adjacent campsite.

I looked at the vehicle which was half as long as a semi truck and appeared as if it had every convenience of home, including a satellite TV antenna on the top.

For a moment, I considered my answer. I mean, I didn't want to tell her the truth. I didn't want to tell her that mommy and daddy would have to mortgage their home and the future of their children to afford such a recreational vehicle.

"We don't have something like that because we want you and your sister to experience true camping."

She gave me a puzzled look.

"You see dear, that is not camping. That is bringing your home into the woods. Camping is becoming one with nature," I said in a tone of voice like that of an ancient wise man passing a precious truth to a young upstart.

"Camping isn't convenient; it's challenging. It's living without air conditioning."

The 5-year-old gave me a blank look.

"Remember last year when we were camping and it rained in the middle of the night and water leaked into the tent and got your sleeping bag all wet?"

She nodded.

"That's camping."

She gave me a bewildered look.

"If you had been in that motorhome over there, you would not have had that experience. You would have been as warm and as dry as if you had been in your own bed at home."

"Daddy, why would I want to sleep in a wet sleeping bag?" she asked.

"You wouldn't."

"So why don't we buy one of those things?"

"Because it is important that you learn what it is like to sleep in a wet sleeping bag. The next time you go camping you'll take along the proper equipment so you won't have to sleep in a wet sleeping bag."

"But if we have one of those things, we'd never have to

worry about being wet."

"Yes dear, but you can't take those RVs everywhere. You can take them to state parks, but if you really want to experience the outdoors, you have to camp in out-of-the-way places, places you can't reach by car."

"Why would we want to go to out-of-the-way places?"

"Because that is where the action is."

"Huh?"

"You see things there you won't see in a populated park."

"Like what?"

"Oh, I don't know. There are certain types of flowers, birds and animals which only live in more remote areas. But more importantly, it's what you won't find. You won't find people, people in big RVs."

"Why don't you want to find people?"

"The people are all right, but it is what they bring along with them that you want to avoid."

She looked up at me with a blank expression.

"Listen," I said putting my finger to my lips. "What do you hear."

She lifted her head and looked around.

"I hear people talking; I hear a car coming down the road, and I hear music," she said.

"Those aren't the sounds of nature," I said.

"They aren't?"

"The chirping sound of a distressed squirrel; the wind rustling leaves; the commotion of a field mouse rummaging through the leaves on the ground—those are the sounds of nature. Hearing PeeWee Herman coming from the TV in the RV next door isn't my idea of experiencing the outdoors!"

The sound of CDs and portable TVs are the sounds of man. And that's why we don't own an RV," I concluded.

"Oh," she said flatly. "I think I'd rather stay dry."

She left and walked over to mom.

"Mommy, why can't we have one of those RDs," she asked her.

"That's RV, honey. We can't afford one, they're very expensive."

"So we'll have to sleep in wet sleeping bags everytime we go camping?"

"Huh?"

With that my daughter walked away. A couple minutes later, I saw her talking to the elderly couple who were sitting by the big RV at the adjacent campsite.

Few minutes later she returned.

"Hey, dad, they said that if my sleeping bag gets wet, I can come stay with them!"

I looked up at the couple, forced an embarrassed smile and turned to my wife.

"Dear, I think it's time we head to the beach."

Worm emancipation is expensive

I have given more worms their freedom than any fisherman I know.

It's not that I intentionally let them loose. It's more that I am a careless guard.

Like I have this tendency to leave the top off the worm container. While I sleep, brave worms slither up from the moist shredded paper and stretch themselves over the edge to the ground below.

The next morning, I don't even notice the top is off. I absentmindedly put it back on, pick up the container, grab my fishing pole and head for the canoe. It isn't until I'm two hours from camp and sitting in my canoe in the middle of a wide lake that I discover the worms are missing.

It doesn't occur to me right away that the worms escaped during the night. Rather I suspect they have slipped out while I was paddling. I get up from my seat, bend down onto my knees and crawl from one end of the canoe to the other, lifting up coats, pushing aside tackleboxes and examing closely my food pack. I once had a worm crawl into my lunch bag. Even though I removed the worm, his respite on my bologna sandwich made eating lunch real interesting.

I guess I don't mind giving worms their freedom. I'd rather let a worm loose than drown him trying to catch fish which have absolutely no interest in eating.

The trouble is worms are expensive.

When it comes to worms, I lack a certain degree of planning. When I'm getting ready for a fishing trip, the last thing I think about is worms. Consequently, I usually forget to buy them. This is what occurred the last time that happened...

"Got the worms?" The Fisherman asks.

"Darn it!" I reply snapping my fingers. "I forgot."

"It's 5 in the morning, where are we going to get worms?"

"Gosh, I don't know." I shrug and walk toward the car.

"Well, I know this tackle shop near the lake. By the time we get up there, it will probably be open," he says.

Sure enough, the bait shop is open when we arrive.

"I'd like a dozen nightcrawlers," I say with a yawn.

"Don't have any," the clerk says with an indifferent tone.

"Got any worms?"

"Well, we have these little red wigglers," he says pointing to worms so small they would fit inside a pencil line.

I turn back to The Fisherman. He glares at me and then nods his head.

"Okay, we'll take a couple dozen."

"That'll be $3.50."

"$3.50!"

103

"Yup, a $1.75 a dozen."

"You got to be crazy. I can get good nightcrawlers for 75 cents a dozen!"

"Don't have any nightcrawlers. All I got is these little wigglers. Super bait, though."

"At that price they ought to be. Heck, I might as well fish with caviar," I say sarcastically.

"Do you want the worms or not?"

I glance back at The Fisherman. His face is turning red.

"OK, I'll take a dozen."

Well, we get out on the lake and drown every one of those dozen worms and catch not one lousy fish. We didn't even have a nibble.

I think this worm-free tradition in the Oakland family will continue into the next generation.

The other day I took my eldest daughter out fishing. I yanked a big nightcrawler out of the container and handed it to her.

"YUCK!" she exclaimed and threw the worm about 10 feet into the air. Poor creature ended up hanging from a small branch in an oak tree.

I then carefully explained that worms, although relatively unattractive, cause humans no harm. The purpose of worms is to entice fish to bite.

Then I gave her another worm. I was pleased that she didn't immediately send it skyward. However, rather than hooking it, she decided the worm was a pleasant distraction from an otherwise boring fishing trip. So she played with it, that is until she inadvertently dropped it over the side of the canoe.

By the time we finished fishing, seven worms had found freedom thanks to my daughter, three worms had drowned, one had actually caught a small perch and one had disappeared somewhere in the canoe.

Worms don't have to worry about their welfare when they go fishing with the Oaklands.

Outdoors brings freedom to...

You know what I like about the outdoors? You can pass gas and nobody cares.

This is a rather delicate subject which I will attempt to address as discreetly as possible.

Gas passing is a real problem.

You see, I never had a gas problem until I started listening to all those health experts telling me I ought to eat more fiber. If I didn't eat fiber, I'd get cancer they said.

Well, I went right down to the grocery store and bought boxes of bran and bushels of vegetables. Every meal I had a double helping of fiber.

Eating vegetables and bran wasn't bad. In fact, I actually got used to eating cereal which tasted like soggy cardboard. The problem was what my body did with all that fiber.

After a feast of fiber, I felt like I had just swallowed a helium balloon which was growing larger and tighter by the minute. I filled up with so much gas, you could have tapped my bellybutton and heated a town in New Hampshire.

Out in the woods such a condition is not a problem. You just let nature take its course and let the winds take care of the consequences.

Even in camp a little indiscretion goes unnoticed. You tend to tolerate a lot more in the fresh air than you do cooped up indoors.

I suspect every animal in the woods has a gas problem now and then. But you'd never know it. I mean, you don't walk down a woodland path, raise your nose and exclaim "Whew, deer farts."

In the woods a man can pass gas without embarrassment, unless he is stalking wild game at the time. If you are standing on a tree stand, your bow drawn and aimed at a 12-point buck, it would be terribly disconcerting if your body let fly a gastrointestinal discharge rivaling the blast of a 12-gauge shotgun.

It is ironic this by-product of our highly desirable high fiber diet is very undesirable. It's not something you'd like to experience in a crowded elevator on a non-stop trip to the 28th floor.

Nor does it add to the ambience of a romantic interlude. I mean, when you are whispering sweet nothings into your beau's ear, another voice, so to speak, would effectively kill the mood.

It is a biological hazard men must confront throughout their years.

I remember suffering during a particularly hard social studies test in high school. The room was so quiet you could hear a pencil crossing a sheet of exam paper. I felt this pressure building within me. The prudent thing would have been to go to the bathroom. But I was a shy kid, a kid who would rather die than raise his hand and ask the teacher– before the entire class– if he could go to the bathroom.

Ten minutes were left before the bell... I loosened my belt and wrapped my legs tightly together.

Five minutes left...My midsection felt as if it was about to explode. I felt so full, I thought my stomach was about to tickle my tonsils. But there was nothing I could do about it. The room was so quiet that even the smallest relief of internal pressure would have been heard by the entire class.

The instant the bell rang, I was out of my seat and out the door. Masked by the commotion in the hall, I released the errant gas in a long, disgustingly loud explosion. Suddenly, the commotion in the hall stopped. Students stood looking around aimlessly as if in a state of shock. I buried my head in a book and slowly walked toward my locker.

I had a similar experience at work.

There I was sitting one on one with the company president. We were going over a speech he would deliver later that day.

I was just about to suggest an introductory joke, when I felt that ominous little tug in my belly. Minutes later the tug had all the

106

subtlety of a depth charge. The deadline was approaching; there was no time to excuse one's self.

Finally, the speech was written. The moment the president left my office, which actually is a small cubicle in a corridor, I let loose.

The fabric walls of my cubicle shuddered.

Books on the shelves toppled.

Suddenly secretaries stopped typing.

Phone conversations abruptly paused.

People in the hallway stopped in mid stride.

Then all eyes turned toward my little cubicle.

A few moments later, the typing resumed, the phone conversations continued and the people once again were walking by.

"I bet beavers never have this problem," I muttered to myself as I buried my head in a book.

NORTHERN LITES CHRONICLES

Sledding to doom

I never thought of sledding as particularly adventurous or dangerous.

I sledded a lot when I was a kid. I remember being wet and cold from numerous spills in the powdery snow. But I don't recall sledding being particularly scary.

The other day, I took my two girls sledding for the first time and the experience forever changed my opinion of this wintertime activity.

I took the girls to a dandy sledding hill at the American Legion Golf Course in Wausau. It was a long, not-too-steep hill, just right for introducing youngsters to the fun of sledding.

We had along with us one of those plastic bobsleds. This was a first for me because I had grown up with the traditional Flexible Flyers and saucers. But parenthood requires you to constantly try new things. Kids aren't much on tradition. What other kids are using is what they want to use, and in most cases the newest type of sled is the most popular.

I was enthusiastic about the prospect of sledding again. As I stood at the top of the hill, I remembered the exhilaration of speeding down a snow covered hill.

I put the little bobsled down and turned to the 3-year-old who had just managed to remove her hat and mittens almost simultaneously. As I fought to get the hat back on her head, the 5-year-old snuck onto the bobsled, and before I realized she was on it, she had pushed herself toward the edge of the hill.

"Watch me, daddy!" she exclaimed.

"Huh?" I turned just in time to see her push the mini bobsled down the slope.

"Omigosh!"

I shot up and took off running down the hill after her. Ever try to run down an icy hill? Fifty yards down the slope my feet shot out from under me and I crashed head first into a snowbank.

I lifted my head out of the snow just in time to witness my daughter slide out of control into a group of adults and children walking up the hill. Some managed to jump out of the way; others fell like tenpins as my daughter slammed into them.

Meanwhile, at the top of the hill, the 3-year-old had positioned herself at the edge of the slope and was about to come down the hill without a sled. Luckily an alert mother grabbed her and plunked her down onto a snowbank.

I got up and brushed snow off my face. I looked down the hill and saw that the 5-year-old was bringing the sled back. I turned and started up the hill. A few yards later, I suddenly realized how much work it is walking up a snow covered slope when you are dressed in a snowmobile suit and are wearing sorrel boots. I felt my leg muscles begin to tighten up. My breathing became more labored.

"Geez, if nothing else this is great aerobic exercise," I

muttered to myself as I felt my heart rate push toward the danger zone.

I stopped to catch my breath and glanced down the hill at my adventurous daughter. Slowly but surely she was pulling the mini bobsled up the hill.

"HEY MISTER LOOK OU....!!!"

I don't remember much of what happened because it happened so fast. But witnesses at the top of the hill said the little boy's sled clipped me behind the knees and that I flew up into the air, did a spread-eagle backflip and landed face down in the snow as the little boy continued down the hill apparently unhurt.

"Dad, are you all right?" my 5-year-old asked as she looked down at me.

"What hit me?" I asked as I tried to get my head out of the fog.

"A kid on a sled. Dad, you've got to watch where you are going," she admonished.

"Don't kids today know how to steer a sled," I complained. "When I was your age I could maneuver sleds around people and trees with ease. Kids don't know nothing nowadays."

My daughter helped me to my feet as a couple of parents came running up to me. I surmised they were the little boy's parents.

"You all right?" they asked, the tone of their voices a mixture of shock and concern.

"I'll live," I replied flatly.

"Too bad you weren't playing football, that would have been a clip worth 15 yards," the man said with a laugh.

I forced a smile and limped up the hill.

When I got to the top, I sat my girls down and told them in no uncertain terms that they were not ready to go down the hill alone.

"You have to learn a few fundamentals first, like steering, how to stop and when to bail out."

"Bail out?" the 3-year-old repeated with a puzzled look.

"That simply means rolling off the sled just before it slams into the side of an oak tree," I explained.

"Why would you want to hit an oak tree?" The 5-year-old asked.

"Forget it kid," I replied. "There aren't any oak trees around here so you don't have to worry about it."

I knelt down next to the little yellow plastic sled. "OK, this time daddy is going down with you, and you watch as he shows you how to steer. Then we'll see about solo sledding."

The 5-year-old's eyes lit up. She wasn't too keen on sledding with daddy, but was willing to endure it if it meant being able to go down alone later on.

"Daddy used to be a pretty mean sledder in his day," I boasted as I sat down in the plastic bobsled and grabbed the cord tied to the front end. "You use this to steer with," I told the 5-year-old as she jumped onto my outstretched legs, causing my already sore knees to painfully pop.

"Easy does it, kid," I moaned.

Then the 3-year-old jumped onto the lap of her sister, the weight causing another sharp surge of pain to shoot through my legs. I began hoping our trip down the hill would be a short one.

"Ready?"

The girls nodded.

"Then here we go."

I gave the sled a push with both arms, and down the slope we went.

"WEEEEEEEE!" The girls screamed.

"Uh, oh," I gasped softly enough so that the girls couldn't hear. I had just realized that with my added weight, the mini bobsled was moving much more swiftly down the hill than I had anticipated. I also discovered it wouldn't steer.

I tugged on the cord with all my strength, but it had no effect on the sled which had suddenly started fishtailing.

"WEEEEEEE!" the girls screamed.

"How the heck do you steer this thing," I yelled to a father

112

walking up the hill. He gave me a startled look, and then suddenly covered his face with his gloves.

I glanced ahead. "Oh, no!"

In front of us was a group of parents and kids.

"GET OUT OF THE WAY!"

As we skidded into the group, I closed my eyes and braced myself for the impact of bodies piling into the little sled. But nothing happened. The little bobsled scooted past some, slid under the legs of others and barely missed a few who at the last moment jumped out of the way.

"Wow!" the 5-year-old exclaimed. "That was neat, daddy!"

I didn't answer. I was trying to get my legs outside the sled so I could dig my feet into the snow and stop us. But I couldn't move my legs because both daughters were sitting on them.

Well, the worst was over, I thought to myself. Soon this winterland rollercoaster ride would be over.

"DADDY! LOOK OUT!" My eldest daughter screamed.

I looked up.

"OH LORDY!"

A few feet in front of us, a few seconds distance, was a man standing in the snow. He didn't see us bearing down on him because he was looking through the viewfinder of a camcorder which was pointed at a little girl sliding down the hill.

There wasn't even time to yell a warning. Our sled slammed into his unsuspecting body like an ax against a tree. The impact overturned our sled, sending my two daughters and me sliding across the snow.

I looked up and saw the man's camcorder shooting skyward. It was turning end over end like an oversized football. Higher and higher it went until it appeared to stop and float momentarily before beginning its descent.

I scrambled to my feet and ran for the fast falling camera like a centerfielder after a high fly ball. I dove and snatched the camera just before impact. I held it above my head as my body crashed into the snow like an airliner making a belly landing on a runway covered with fire-retardant foam. When I finally stopped most of my body was under the snow.

I got up, spit the snow from my mouth and wiped my face with one hand. In the other hand was the undamaged camcorder, still running.

It was a $1,000 catch, but no one cheered. Instead the man got up, limped over to me, yanked the camcorder from my hands while expressing his displeasure in words unprintable here.

"Hey! Think of the bright side," I said trying to console him. "You've got a perfect entry for *America's Funniest Home Videos.*"

He wasn't amused.

As he stomped away, I motioned to my girls to head for the car. Looking up the hill at all those angry faces, I decided to get out of there before anyone recognized me.

"Let's go get some hot chocolate. It might settle my nerves," I told the girls as I picked up the bobsled and started off through the snow.

Every winter it's mitten mania

I'll be the first to admit outdoor clothing is pretty darn sophisticated.

I mean, you have coats which supposedly let moisture from the body escape while keeping out moisture from the air. You have long underwear that will keep you warm no matter how cold it gets.

But if we are so smart, how come we can't design mittens kids can't lose?

I swear, we buy our 3-year-old mittens and they are gone within a week. Eventually we'll find one, but one mitten is as useful as no mittens at all.

Buy mittens with strings attached, you say.

Mittens with strings is a nice idea which just doesn't survive your average 3-year-old. Invariably as you struggle to get the kid's coat on, the string gets tangled up and snaps. Or the child merrily pulls on one mitten until the other is completely through the coat.

If you attach the mittens with steel chain, perhaps it would last a season.

There are other problems with mittens.

Buying them is a real chore.

You go into a store and find yourself confronted with racks containing millions and millions of mittens, all joined together by little plastic cords.

I hate those cords.

The last time I tried to buy mittens for my youngest daughter, she fought furiously as I tried to get a pair of mittens on her. After considerable effort, I finally got both mittens on her.

"How do they feel," I asked as I tried to catch my breath.

Instead of giving me a simple affirmative or negative response, she jerked her arms apart causing that little nylon cord to rip the rings right off the mittens.

I sheepishly looked around then threw the damaged mittens under a display rack.

I suppose most people have little trouble finding the proper size of mitten for their youngsters. I have one heckuva time. I have a kid with one-of-a-kind hands. Mittens are either too big— fine if she wants to go into boxing— or too small— fine if you're willing to bathe her hands in Vaseline before putting them on.

I'm sorry if the following comment seems unAmerican, but I think it is stupid to put images of Mickey Mouse or Bugs Bunny or the Sesame Street Gang on mittens. What happens is a kid insists daddy buy him Mickey Mouse mittens, even though out of a million such mittens in the store, you can't find one that fits properly.

If mitten manufacturers are so hep on putting pictures on mittens, they ought to figure out a way to put a picture of the mitten's owner on the outside. Wouldn't that be great. You'd never have to worry about your kid bringing home the wrong mittens from school. Lost and found would be a piece of cake.

In this age of the microchip, you'd think someone could come up with a homing mitten. Stitch a little transmitter in the lining so that when the little tyke loses the mittens, you can just press a button to activate the homing device and track the mittens down.

My kids are great for flinging mittens. Boots and coats usually end up on the floor. But mittens can be thrown all sorts of places. We've found them behind chairs, on top of the china cabinet and in the kitchen sink. We even found a mitten half eaten by the garbage disposal.

And we quickly learned it is a waste of time asking children where their mittens are.

"Darling, we're late, where are your mittens?"

"I don't know," my 5-year-old says.

"When did you last have them on?"

"I can't remember," she replies.

"When did you last go outside?"

"Yesterday morning."

"Did you have your mittens on?"

"I don't know."

"Were you hands cold?"

"No."

"Then you must have had your mittens on. Where did you go when you came inside?"

"I can't remember, daddy."

"Have you seen your sister's mittens?"

"Nope."

We later found the mittens under the covers of her bed. She had forgotten she had tried to put the mittens on her doll.

I tell you, I'd work on the problem of mittens myself, but I don't have time during the winter. I'm too busy looking for my own gloves.

Figure skating becomes fatal skating

I should have seen it coming.

I just should have said no.

Instead I just smiled and told my eldest daughter, yes, Santa Claus might bring you ice skates for Christmas.

I guess it was my daughter's enthusiasm which kept me from considering exactly what I had agreed to.

You see, Santa brings more than skates. Santa brings with them a requirement that daddy teach his little girl how to properly use the new skates.

It doesn't matter that daddy hasn't touched a pair of ice skates since sixth grade.

It doesn't matter that daddy may fall and do permanent damage to his rather brittle and inflexible body.

It's a daddy's responsibility.

I felt lucky I didn't have sons. Instead of figure skating I'd be looking at the inside of a hockey rink. After watching some neighborhood hockey games played by pint-sized puck chasers, I was convinced that such instruction would have resulted in my premature death– a hockey puck between the eyes or a stick to the throat.

Christmas came and sure enough my daughter got her wish. Under the tree was a pair of little, white figure skates.

A couple of days later, I took my daughter to the neighborhood rink. To my amazement, she did quite well. However, I didn't do so well. When you aren't wearing skates, it is somewhat awkward keeping up with a kid wearing skates.

Being the good dad, I stopped by the local ice skate shop the following day and purchased a pair of black figure skates. "Heck, it is probably just like riding a bike," I said to myself as I sat in the warming house. "Once you learn, you never forget."

I felt pretty confident, mainly because I was able to walk my skates across the warming house floor without taking a nosedive.

"Now daddy is a little rusty at this," I told my daughter, who was right behind me. "He has to go a little slow."

Holding on to the warming house doorway, I eased out onto the ice. Slowly I let go of the door, which instantly slammed shut. For a moment, I just stood there hoping that my body would remember how to skate because it was apparent my conscious mind had forgotten.

Suddenly, I felt a pair of hands in the small of my back. Before I could turn around, my daughter gave me an abrupt push. "OOOOOOOOHHH NOOOOOOO!" I screamed as I flailed my arms wildly in an attempt to regain my balance.

I soon realized I was gaining speed. What I had failed to notice while walking across the rink in street shoes was that the ice sloped gradually away from the warming house. I also realized I had absolutely no idea how to stop.

My legs were going any direction but straight; my arms were whipping around like two huge propellers, and my body was jerking side to side like a disco dancer with fire ants up his polyester pants.

Suddenly I realized my out of control body was careening right for a small girl who was skating arm in arm with her mother. "LOOK OUT BELOW"

The lady screamed and pushed her little girl out of the way.

In trying to avoid the collision, I dug the tip of my left skate into the ice, which caused me to go into an abrupt airborne spin. I was later told by witnesses that in that brief second I left the ice, and a moment before I slammed broadside into that woman, I looked sort of like a freaked-out Brian Boitano doing a triple axel.

Down the woman went with me right on top of her, my face buried in her coat. People gathered around us. They looked stunned and just stood there slowly shaking their heads.

With a little help from the onlookers, I managed to get back on my skates. The lady got up, gave me the nastiest look I have ever witnessed and skated off to her daughter.

I spotted my own daughter still standing by the warming house doorway, her hands covering her face. I slowly turned toward her, took two small steps and fell right on my tailbone.

My daughter came skating up to me.

"Daddy are you all right?"

Fighting back the tears, I replied. "I'll live. I may never be able to walk straight again, but I'll live."

I crawled across the ice to the snowbank and with my skates firmly cushioned by the deep snow, I walked back to the warming house. "We'll continue your lesson tomorrow," I told my daughter as she pulled off my skates. She had to pull them off as my back was in no condition to allow me to bend over and unlace them.

As we were walking home— actually my daughter was walking, I was limping—we saw a teenage boy cross the school grounds on a pair of cross country skis.

"Gee, daddy, that looks like fun." my daughter said. "Will you teach me how to do that?"

"Next year, darling, maybe next year," I groaned.

Get to bed or else!

My kids have developed a marvelously effective strategy for staying up past their bedtimes.

It's called "Read Me a Story."

One of the things I wasn't warned about when I decided to become a parent was the battles that would occur around bedtime.

I mean, the kids can be well-behaved all day, but mention that it is time for bed and they instantly become, as we modern parents say, behavior problems.

"I don't want to go to bed!" My eldest daughter says as her

119

sister jumps off a chair and runs to hide behind the couch.

I shut off the TV. "Come on girls, let's brush our teeth and get our jammies on." As I leave the livingroom, I hear the TV come back on.

"No more TV, it is way past your bed time," I scold as I return to the livingroom and slam down the off switch of the TV.

The 5-year-old doesn't move from the recliner as I go hunting for the 3-year-old. I pull the little tyke from behind the couch and carry her off to the bathroom. The 5-year-old gets up from the recliner, not to come to the bathroom, but to turn on the TV. She knows she has me. If I come back to turn off the TV, the 3-year-old will escape from the bathroom and hide somewhere else.

I finish up with the 3-year-old and come after her sister. I pull her from the recliner and carry her out of the room as I once again shut off the TV.

As I drop her off at the bathroom, I hear the TV come on again. I race back to the livingroom only to find the 3-year-old sitting in the recliner watching *Mr. Ed* on TV. My wife and I thought it was so cute when our littlest one taught herself how to turn the TV on. Now it isn't so cute.

I scoop up the 3-year-old, shut off the TV and carry her back to the bathroom where I expect to find the 5-year-old. But she isn't there. I look in the bedroom. She isn't there either. Suddenly I hear the TV come on.

I put the 3-year-old into bed. "Don't you dare get out of bed!" I threaten. Then I leave to fetch her sister. Like a snarling grizzly, I charge down the hall toward the recliner. In an instant the 5-year-old is out of the chair and running toward the bedroom.

"Now go to sleep," I say with more than a little irritation in my voice.

"Daddy, read us a story," the 5-year-old says.

"It's way past your bedtime."

"Please, just one story."

You see this is where kids have got their parents. They don't know why, but they know their parents will always honor a request to read a story.

The reason is their parents will feel terribly guilty if they don't. It's like if you don't read them a story, it will somehow affect their ability to do well in school...

Jane is a straight A student because her parents read to her every night. Dick's parents never read stories to him and look what happened. Dick is the crime boss of the second grade— he can't read or write, but boy can he terrorize a neighborhood.

So no matter how exhausted you are and no matter what time it is, you feel obligated to pick out a story and read it.

Naturally you pick out the shortest story you can find.

"I don't want that one," my 5-year-old says bluntly.

"Look, I let you stay up way past your bedtime..."

"I don't like that story...read me this one instead!" she demands as she points to a book that would take an hour and a half to read.

"That's too long," I reply pulling out a different book which has the two attributes of a good bedtime book— large pictures and few words.

"I don't want that one, I want..."

"How about this one..."

"No!"

"This one?"

"No!"

In the process of going through her entire library of books, I neglect to keep an eye on the 3-year-old who has left her bed and snuck out of the room.

"Well, how about..." I pause as I hear sound all too familiar in the Oakland household. "Hey! Turn off that TV!" I shout.

I race out of the room, grab the 3-year-old, unplug the TV and return to the bedroom only to find that in my absence the 5-year-old has removed every book from her bookshelf and has deposited every one of them on her bed.

I tuck in the 3-year-old, clean the books off the 5-year-old's bed and pick up the smallest storytime book I can find and read it so fast I sound like Mr. Rogers on speed.

"There, good night!"

"I want a drink of water!" The 3-year-old demands.

"OK, OK."

Heck, you can't expect a kid to go to bed thirsty so I go to the kitchen, get a glass of water and give it to her. She then takes one sip so small it would fit inside an eye dropper.

"Good night," I sigh.

Forty five minutes since I first announced it was bedtime, I finally accomplished the task. I find my recliner, put my beer on the table next to it and get ready to enjoy what little is left of the evening.

Before I can take my first sip of beer, I'm asleep. Battle fatigue.

Puzzles are a real pain for parents

Jigsaw puzzles are challenging.

But when you have small children around the house, the challenge is not putting the pieces together, but finding them.

The other day, I bought my 5-year-old a 70-piece Mickey Mouse puzzle. I figured it would take the kid most of the afternoon to put it together. Wrong. She dumped the pieces onto the table and proceeded to put it together herself... in under 15 minutes. She promptly lost interest in the puzzle and went off to hassle her younger sister.

And there I sat staring at $8.95 down the tubes.

I put the puzzle away and went off to break up a fight between the two girls.

A couple days later, I discovered my eldest daughter and a

friend had pulled the puzzle out of the toy chest and had put it together. Then they had flicked the board so that the pieces scattered all over the toy room. Then they left.

Being a patient parent and not wanting to strain my vocal cords any more than they had already been strained that day, I began to pick up the pieces and do the puzzle myself.

I didn't mind. It did my ego good to see that I could still put together a puzzle, albeit a Mickey Mouse puzzle. The last puzzle I had put together was a Playboy Centerfold puzzle back when I was in college. I tell you, it was quite an experience for a young man to put together a naked woman piece by piece. It took me half the night just looking for her navel. Shortly after completing it, the puzzle disappeared. I suspected, but could never prove, that my girlfriend torched it.

Unfortunately, the Mickey Mouse puzzle could never be completed. It was a 70-piece puzzle with only 68 pieces.

"Hey! Where's the rest of the puzzle?" I yelled to my eldest daughter who was watching TV in the livingroom.

She replied with the most often heard phrase from a child's lips: "I dunno."

"What do you mean you don't know. You got it out, and I know all the pieces were there when I last put it away. Think!"

She replied with the second most often heard phrase from a child's lips: "My sister did it."

"No I didn't" the 3-year-old protested.

"Yes you did!" the 5-year-old shot back.

"You're a dummy head!" the little one countered.

"I don't care who took the pieces. I just want to know where they are!" I shouted as I ran out of the playroom to separate my daughters who were at that moment acting like the main card at an All-Star Wrestling Match.

"OK girls, you're going to help me find the missing pieces. One looks like Mickey's ear and the other one is part of a blue wall."

"Why do I have to look, she took them," the 5-year-old said as she cast an angry glance at her sister.

"I don't care. You're both helping me look for them," I said sternly as I dragged both kids back into the playroom.

Well, we found pieces of toys which had been missing for months, but no pieces of the puzzle were to be found. I swear the kids must have eaten them.

"Don't you realize, a 70-piece puzzle with only 68 pieces is no good," I cried out.

The kids just gave me a blank look. It was the same blank look I got when I tried to explain that Candyland without all the cards is no longer a viable game.

"It's not like your Crayons. I mean, if you lose a red Crayon, you can still use the other colors. But if you lose Mickey's nose, the puzzle just doesn't work," I explained to my eldest daughter. Her only response was to ask where her Crayons were so she could go draw.

Completeness is not in a kid's nature.

I remember when my eldest daughter was only 2, we bought her a simple, five-piece wooden puzzle. It was a fairly expensive toy. But we delighted when she was first able to fit the balloons in the balloon slots and the clown in the clown slot.

Two days later one of the balloons turned up missing.

To this day, we have not found it.

Puzzle pieces must be absorbed into the earth.

Maybe there is a gremlin who roams the world stealing puzzle pieces with the hope some day of putting together a puzzle of a million unrelated pieces.

I tell you one thing, in the Oakland household there will be no puzzles more than 100 pieces unless an armed guard stands at the door while it is being put together.

Does daddy play with dollies?

I had a strange dream the other night. While I'm not one who attaches significance to dreams, I admit this particular dream has me worried that it holds some subconscious message.

The dream begins in a park. I am jogging along a winding sidewalk which borders a wide, green lawn stretching as far as I can see.

I feel good and healthier than I have for a long time. No matter how fast I run, no matter how steep the incline, I don't get winded. My body runs with a machine-like rhythm— something I never experience in real life.

Looking around, I see little pockets of people playing. In the distance, I see young men playing softball. Just behind a little knoll, a group of girls, perhaps coeds from a nearby college, play a giggly game of volleyball.

The sidewalk I am running on takes a turn and heads directly toward the volleyball game and the softball contest beyond it. As I approach, the girls closest to me turn their attention away from the game and toward me. Soon all the girls are watching me watching them.

They are beautiful young women, just like you see in soda pop or beer commercials. Their bodies are lean and athletic, yet their faces are warm and almost child like.

A tall, blonde girl in a bright pink tank top and white short shorts smiles at me and beckons me to join her and the other girls in the game. Two girls break from the group and run toward me. They grab my arms and pull me toward the court.

I want to join them, but my body pulls me away. My arms suddenly become possessed with a strength I've never known before and I break from their grasp and run away.

I glance back and see the girls giggling and pointing at me as if I were some sexy movie star like Tom Cruise or Mel Gibson.

Just ahead is the softball game.

125

The players again look like actors in a beer commercial—you know, they move like professional athletes, yet are dressed like Yuppies on a weekend.

One of the players motions me to come over to the dugout. When I approach, he hands me a bat and points to the plate. The home team cheers, while the players out in the field look worried. The guy in left field starts moving toward the fence; the pitcher nervously tosses the ball in his hand, and the infielders tighten their stances.

The pitcher throws a high arching ball. I swing and I feel the bat connect hard into the ball and watch as it sails high into the sky. I drop the bat and take off for first. The ball is still in the air as I round first base.

As I approach second base, a little girl suddenly appears out of right field, a girl who resembles my 5-year-old daughter. For some odd reason, I stop running and turn toward her.

"Daddy, can you hold my Cabbage Patch Doll," she says sweetly as she hands me the little brown haired doll. I take the doll from her and take off running.

Suddenly I feel very winded.

I look up and the second baseman is looking at me strangely, as if he has never seen a ballplayer come into second base carrying a Cabbage Patch doll.

The ball appears from nowhere, slams into the second baseman's glove, which brushes against my shoulder as my right foot approaches the bag.

The second baseman backs away. The other players just stare. Some smirk, some whisper, some just shake their heads as I slowly walk off the field, the doll dangling from my right hand.

With each step the vigor vanishes. It's as if my body is aging by the minute instead of the year. The muscles in my arms, which were tight and well defined just moments before, are now covered with a layer of fat.

I amble up the sidewalk and past the volleyball game. The

girls are as bouncy and voluptuous as before, yet this time, they don't notice me. Even when they are looking right at me, they don't notice me.

Then the tall blonde who before had beckoned me to join the game, stops and points at me and begins to giggle. She taps one of her girlfriends on the shoulder and points at me again. No, not at me, but at the Cabbage Patch Doll cradled in my right arm. The two girls laugh harder and then turn back to their game.

I suddenly feel terribly embarrassed, as if I had committed the most atrocious thing a man could do—to suddenly give up his manhood.

I look back at the young girls volleying the ball over the net and the men playing softball. They all are so young, so full of energy and so physically appealing. Then I look down at my protruding belly and glance at my rounded shoulders. And then I stare down at the doll.

I throw the doll down. Suddenly I feel a rush of energy and a tightening of my muscles. I watch as the definition returns to my arms and thigh muscles, and I feel my lungs and heart strengthen.

But then the doll gets up, walks toward me and leaps into my arms. The instant it lands, my strength and my youth flow away as if released by a dam gate.

Again I throw down the doll.

It jumps right back.

I throw it down again and try to run. But it follows, passes me and jumps into my arms again.

Once more I throw it down....

It was at that point, that my wife awakened me. Apparently I had been throwing the pillow at her repeatedly. As she turned to go back to sleep, I looked up at the ceiling and thought about those beautiful young girls and those athletic young men. I turned on my side and was about to return to sleep when I was startled by my 5-year-old daughter, who was standing in front of me and holding her Cabbage Patch doll.

127

"Daddy, I had a bad dream, can my dolly and I come into your bed, please....

"Come on in, but leave the doll behind," I groaned.

Peaceful dinners by progressive processing

Food processors create peaceful dinners.

They are made for parents who have trouble getting junior to eat.

Take for instance, suppertime at the Oakland house.

"Eat your peas!" I yell at the 3-year-old who is taking individual peas, putting them on a spoon and shooting them at the 5-year-old across the table.

"How many bites?" she asks.

"A hundred!"

"Two bites?"

That's her favorite line. She could have a plate filled to the edge with food and still insist that two bites would satisfy all her nutritional needs.

Meanwhile, on the other side of the table, the 5-year-old has eaten her peas and fruit, but absolutely refuses to touch her meat or potatoes.

"You must eat your meat or else you won't grow up big and strong," I tell her softly, repeating the same line my parents used to give me. Unfortunately it has the same impact. My daughter just sits there using a fork to push chunks of meat around in the mashed potatoes.

Anyway, this battle of wits continues for the rest of the meal. The 3-year-old throws potatoes on the floor, and the 5-year-old hides a piece of meat under her plate. Soon their plates are clean—not because they ate anything, but because they managed to relocate the meal onto the table, floor and down the inside of their shirts.

A young mother once told me the way to get around this was to serve them one food item at a time. You give them meat and when they have eaten it, you give them the vegetable.

"It is a lot less messy because the kids have less to mess with," she said.

It sounded like an ideal strategy. Unfortunately, there was one drawback. Mommy and daddy didn't get a chance to eat their dinner because they were constantly passing food to the kids.

It seemed as if my wife and I were doomed to dinner distress. We either got indigestion from yelling at the kids to clean their plates, or we got heartburn from serving the kids their dinner piecemeal.

Then one day, my eldest daughter fell down on the ice skating rink. She said the fall caused her teeth to hurt. Careful inspection revealed no injury to the teeth, nevertheless she was adamant that her teeth hurt every time she chewed.

I figured she was faking it so I called her bluff. "OK, if your teeth hurt, I'll just grind up your dinner."

Well, she thought that was just a marvelous idea. My wife gave me one of those "now look what you have done" looks.

"Are you sure?" I asked.

"My teeth hurt, grind up the food!" She replied without hesitation.

So I prepared what I thought was an absolutely delicious ham, rice and mixed vegetable dinner. Everything for once was done to perfection. The ham was cooked in a flavorful pineapple sauce; the rice was steamed to a delicate softness, and the vegetables were firm and colorful.

I neatly arranged each item on everyone's plate and summoned the family to the kitchen. I figured once my daughter saw how nice and tasty dinner looked, she would change her mind about the grinding business.

"Daddy, you promised you'd grind it up," the 5-year-old said pushing her plate toward the center of the table.

"OK, OK" I sighed.

I grabbed the plate and with a fork, dumped the entire contents into the bowl of the food processor and flicked the switch. Instantly the three part dinner become one part mush.

"Try to think of it as Chinese," I said scooping the mass of mush onto her plate. Except for flecks of color from the mixed vegetables, the concoction looked rather bland.

My wife took one look at it and groaned.

"Maybe I should shut off the lights," I suggested.

Instead of answering, my wife just looked down at her plate.

I figured the kid would refuse to eat it and I'd end up throwing out the whole mess.

But to my surprise, the kid gobbled it up. I mean, she took her spoon and in several minutes her plate was clean.

What was even more amazing was the 3-year-old piped up and demanded her supper be food processorized.

"Comeon kid, you don't want me to turn your aesthetically pleasing meal into something resembling the inside of a garbage disposal," I suggested.

"I want mine just like hers," she said sternly.

I should have known. I mean, what one sister gets, the other must have regardless of what it tastes or looks like. Unfortunately, once the 3-year-old gets what the 5-year-old is having, she finds out she doesn't like it and ends up not touching it.

"OK," I sighed "I'll grind yours up too."

I took her plate and scraped off everything into the food processor– the tender ham, tasty rice and colorful vegetables– flicked on the switch and turned it into something not of this Earth.

I slopped the slimy looking entree back onto the plate and handed it to the youngster. The kid took her spoon and cleaned it right off the plate.

"I think I'm on to something here," I said to my wife. "I

mean, kids don't care what their food looks like. They are more interested in taste and convenience. The food processor doesn't change the taste of the food— except for combining dissimilar items into a single mass— and it certainly makes things more convenient. The kids don't have three different foods staring up and intimidating them. They have just one.

"And this relieves them of having to cut with a knife, thus making the meal a whole lot safer for all concerned. It helps us too. We have less silverware to wash. Because we can get an entire dinner on one plate, there will be fewer dishes to clean..."

"Donald, you can't serve your children mush all the time," my wife protested.

"Why not? We could have turkey mush on Monday; beef mush on Tuesday; fish mush on Friday..."

"Donald, think of the long term consequences. Our kids will never be able to eat in a restaurant. Can you imagine them asking the waitress to send their meal back to the kitchen to be pureed?" She asked.

"But consider it as a short term solution. As the children get older and see other kids eating, they'll give up the mush. I mean, I don't think any kid would want their McDonald's Happy Meal mushed."

My wife gave me a weird look and left the table.

I began having thoughts of publishing a series of cookbooks:

"Oakland's Oriental Mush"

"Parents Guide to Food Processing"

"Shop Smart; Chop Smart— How to fool your kids into eating right"

"Don's 30-minute Daily Diet— Mush your way to a slimmer, trimmer you"

"Great Gruel— Recipes for the Modern Mom"

Daughters and databases don't mix

Computers are supposed to make life easier.

Well, that ain't the case if small kids are around...

"Daddy, can I use your 'puter," my eldest daughter asks as she bursts into my basement office.

"That's COMputer and the answer is no. Daddy is busy writing."

"But daddy you promised."

"Not now, dear."

"Why not," she says as her hands move toward the keyboard.

"Don't touch anything!" I tell her as I catch her hand by the wrist.

"But, daddy," she whines.

"No."

"Please."

"No."

"Just a minute, daddy," she pleads.

"Oh, all right. You ruined my train of thought anyway."

"What train?" She gives me a funny look.

"Never mind."

I lift her onto my lap.

"Now don't touch anything until I say..."

Before I can say another word, her inquisitive little fingers are running across the keyboard. Her index finger skips onto the "Delete" key. Instantly the screen goes black and 25 paragraphs of arduous writing disappear into electronic heaven."

"AAAAAAAAARGH!

"What's wrong daddy?" she asks innocently.

"You erased my story!" I groan.

"Erase? How could I erase anything, daddy. I don't have a pencil with an eraser."

"Never mind. Just don't touch any more keys."

"Sorry daddy."

It's my own darn fault. I introduced her to the computer before she could read and before she understood what a computer is. To her, it is a TV that you can write on.

I felt pretty good as I watched her learn how to get in and out of a program for kids, a piece of software designed to teach the basics of reading.

But now I'm worried.

Someday she'll sneak down to my office, walk over to my computer and turn it on. Then instead of putting in the disk containing her "educational" program, she will put in my word processing disk.

When she doesn't see the funny little rabbit which guides her through her various "educational exercises," she'll become confused. She'll start pressing keys. She'll inadvertently pull down menus on my Mac. She'll innocently select from one menu a command called "erase disk."

And when the dialog box comes up "Do you really want to erase your disk?" she'll just assume it is another game and press OK.

Thousands upon thousands of bits of information will perish without as much as a whimper. Months and months of work will be for naught.

She'll just stare at the blank screen and wonder where her little rabbit is.

It's a risk I have to take. I mean, tomorrow's students will be learning on computers. Computers will be in their homes, classrooms and offices. I figure the sooner a child becomes familiar with a computer, the more comfortable he or she will be with computers in school.

The trouble is computers are so unforgiving. They don't care if the user is a child or an adult. They don't care if the user is just learning or is an expert. You play by their rules or you don't play at all.

I mean, there isn't a computer around that will flash a message like this:

"Your command sequencing is not indicative of adult behavior. Therefore, unless you can enter the Adult User Code Number, any command you enter will not be executed until adult supervision is indicated."

Or something like this...

"If you don't get off this computer, we'll tell your mommy!"

Of course, there will also be the inevitable conflict between amusement and business...

"I gotta use my computer," I tell my daughter who is sitting at my computer playing some wild game.

"Just a minute, dad," she says without looking away from the screen. "I just have to find the Treasure of Sandubal and then rescue the prince from the evil king..."

"Well, the king will have to wait, I have a report due tomorrow morning."

"Just a minute, dad."

"You said that 20 minutes ago."

"Comeon dad, give me a break."

Unbeknownst to either of us, my youngest daughter has entered the room. Silently she walks up behind us as we continue to argue. Suddenly she reaches out and slams her hand down on the keyboard. The screen goes blank. My eldest daughter screams and turns to attack her sister, who, sensing she has done something bad, has made a beeline for the door.

"I'm gonna kill you," my eldest daughter says as she takes off after her sister.

I yell up to my wife, to catch the kids at the top of the stairs before complete sibling mayhem breaks out.

I tell you, having a computer around the house does not make things easier.

134

I'm a kid tracker extraordinaire

I don't like to brag, but I'm a good tracker— Not of animals or criminals, but of kids in stores.

My two daughters are forever wandering off while my wife and I shop. Like if we don't strap them into the cart, within two minutes of being in the store they're gone.

When we go shopping, we spend half the time looking for the goods we need and half the time looking for one or both of our kids.

So it was out of necessity I became an expert kid tracker.

Tracking kids is not unlike tracking down wild animals. And as a public service to parents everywhere, I'd like to share my expertise.

Years ago, kid tracking was relatively uncommon, except in large stores with numerous departments. The reason was store shelves were low and parents could usually see the entire store if they got up on their toes.

Nowadays, store owners are stacking merchandise right up to the ceiling. Heck, in some grocery stores, merchandise is warehoused between the top shelves and the ceiling.

Your child could be a few yards from you and you'd never see him.

Some parents just yell out the kid's name.

I've found that ineffective.

Other people in the store give you funny looks. Then their expressions turn angry because you're disturbing their shopping.

Secondly, there's a 50-50 chance your kid won't hear you above the Muzak and announcements over the public address system.

Thirdly, if your child did hear you, there is a 99 percent chance he would ignore you. Hearing you would only reassure the tyke that you are still around and that he has plenty of time to continue his exploration.

The best alternative is to forego looking for that special bargain and go after the little wanderer.

Here's a guide to effective kid tracking.

Listen— Before you go anywhere, stop and listen for a minute. Nine times out of ten, the sound of a crashing dish or a clothes rack toppling over pinpoints the location of your child.

Look—Check aisles immediately adjacent to your location. My experience has been that most of the time the child knows where you are even though you have no idea where the child is. They usually don't stray more than an aisle or two from you.

However, sometimes you don't realize the child is gone until you have moved to another aisle. Tracking down the child becomes more difficult because the trail is less fresh.

Think— Just like a deer hunter tries to think like a deer when tracking down his prey, you should think like a kid when trying to find your child.

The obvious first choice is the toy department. Go immediately to the toys which are the most expensive or the toys which easily break. I'd also recommend trying the games section. Children love to open boxes and watch all the pieces fall out.

But if your child isn't in the toy section, try the electronics department. Often the sounds and sights of the electronics department resemble a toy department. When you think about it what are stereos and radios but adult toys.

If your child isn't there, run as fast as you can to the china and glassware displays. Anything that can shatter has a magnetic attraction to anyone under the age of 10.

Be creative— Try to think of things a child can get into that would A) cost loads of money to replace, or B) cause you the most embarrassment if broken.

I once found one of my daughters by shelves of deodorant. She was taking the lids off spray deodorant cans and spraying the contents along the display.

If all else fails— Try the checkouts because that is where the candy is.

Many times I have caught my 5-year-old handing a pack of gum or M & Ms to a cashier, even though she doesn't have the money to pay for it.

I'll conclude with one other tip for parents of chronic wanderers.

Upon entering the store, get your child a small package of M & Ms. Allow him to open the package and eat the candy while you shop.

Most of the time, the child will rip open too much of the bag, allowing M & Ms to periodically fall out. When the kid wanders off, you merely follow the trail of brightly colored M & Ms on the floor.

Someday I plan to produce a video providing comprehensive instruction in the art of child tracking. The more skillful parents are in finding their children, the better it will be for them and all the other shoppers who either don't have children or are afraid to bring them into the store.

Family food fights flare up

In our home, the garbage disposal eats better than half the people in the world.

It seems the concept of cleaning your plate is lost on our kids and the younger generation in general.

Maybe it is a result of our preoccupation with dieting and an abhorrent philosophy that it is all right to leave food on your plate.

"Don't feel guilty leaving half a steak on your plate, your body contour is more important," they tell us.

Hey, a good cow died for that steak, the least you can do is eat it.

Anyway, the bottomline of all this is dinner around the

Oakland household has become battleground.

"Will you please finish your peas!" I yell at my eldest daughter.

"And you, stop playing with your potatoes," I tell my 3-year-old as I watch her whip a spoonful of my finest mashed potatoes onto the floor."

"Don't you realize a family of four in China could make a Thanksgiving dinner out of what you are wasting," I continue. The girls respond with blank stares.

Heck, that line always worked with my generation. The way my mother made it sound, I was the root cause of all world hunger.

I've tried other tactics.

I've tried yelling and threatening.

"Eat your spinach or go to your room!"

The kids don't pay any attention.

"EAT YOUR SPINACH OR GO TO YOUR ROOM"

The eldest daughter looks up, puts a fork into the spinach and twists it around a few times.

"OK, I'M GOING TO COUNT TO FIVE, IF I DON'T SEE SPINACH HEADING TOWARD YOUR MOUTH, YOU ARE HEADING TO YOUR ROOM FOR THE REST OF THE NIGHT."

She continues fiddling with the green leafy vegetable.

"ONE"

She lifts a leaf, but quickly puts it back down on the plate. It lands right on top of the mashed potatoes.

"TWO"

She looks up at me with an expression of innocence and defiance.

"THREE"

She lifts the leaf of spinach out of the mashed potatoes.

"FOUR"

She moves the fork in the direction of her mouth.

"FIVE"

One forkful of spinach enters her mouth. She chews it and

chews it and chews it.

"OK, lets eat some more."

She continues chewing.

"I'LL GIVE YOU TO A COUNT OF FIVE OR ELSE..."

And thus the process begins again.

Such a strategy doesn't work with the 3-year-old.

"EAT YOUR SPINACH"

She looks up, her lips tighten into a pout and her face turns red.

"I'LL COUNT TO FIVE OR YOU'RE GOING TO BED"

That ultimatum is met with a screaming, food-throwing temper tantrum which results in nothing being eaten and mom's and dad's dinner being ruined.

Another problem is what I call the "Keeping Up With The Jones" syndrome. What daughter A has, daughter B must have regardless of whether she likes it or not.

My 3-year-old is great at this.

"Daddy, I want salad," she demands.

"Darling, you never eat salad," I reply softly.

"I want salad, pleeeze," she says pointing to the salad bowl in front of my eldest daughter.

"NO. You won't eat it."

"I WANT SALAD" she screams.

"NO." I reply, holding my ground.

"I WANT SALAD."

"NO SALAD, HAVE PEAS INSTEAD." I offer as a compromise.

One thing parents quickly learn is that 3-year-olds don't compromise.

"I WANT SALAD."

"OK, here have some of your sister's salad," I tell her as I grab the bowl from in front of my eldest daughter and fork a few bits of lettuce onto the 3-year-old's plate.

"I WANT MY OWN SALAD." she says pushing the plate away.

"Dad, you took some of my salad. I want it back!" The 5-year-old complains.

"Hey, you never finish your salad anyway," I counter.

That doesn't matter to her. And by taking some of the salad away, I have given her an excuse not to eat her salad because in someway I have violated the integrity of the serving.

In the end, the 5-year-old doesn't eat her salad because she is mad at daddy; the 3-year-old doesn't eat her salad because she believes it is a hand-me-down; daddy doesn't eat his salad because he has indigestion and mommy doesn't eat her salad because she is mad at daddy for not being able to get the kids to eat.

I tell you, around the Oakland household, dinner is a regular war zone.

The Rifleman and the hornet

When you get to be my age, you'll cherish any moment of glory no matter how brief or insignificant.

Take for instance, a recent battle in which a hornet made me a hero.

Nothing strikes fear into a family more than the discovery of a hornet in the house. Outside you don't worry about hornets or bees because you know given half a chance, they'll eventually fly off. But trapped inside a house, a hornet becomes a caged marauder growing meaner by the minute.

Unlike a housefly, hornets fight back. That makes trying to get rid of them with a flyswatter a more challenging and dangerous endeavor. In fact, it is darnright foolhardy because nine times out of ten, a flyswatter misses its target the first time.

Nor can you use a rolled up newspaper against a hornet. Once I tried whacking a wasp with the Daily News only to find the wasp was very much alive in a crevice created by the folds in the paper. He shot out of that rolled up paper like a scrambling Air Force fighter and came at me with stinger charged. Had I not locked myself in the bathroom for the next half hour, he would have stung me for sure.

Anyway, let me get back to my story.

It was a hot and terribly humid afternoon. My two daughters and I were having lunch in a sweltering kitchen. Suddenly I heard that distinctive buzzing and quickly glanced around the room. The buzzing stopped. I breathed a sigh of relief and went to pick up my peanut butter and jelly sandwich. I was just about to take a bite when to my horror, I found a hornet sitting on a glob of jelly.

I threw the sandwich down and yelled to the girls to get out of the kitchen as fast as they could.

"A bee, daddy, a bee!" The 3-year-old said watching the hornet swoop down and make a low pass over the potato salad.

I grabbed her and quickly carried her into the livingroom. Meanwhile, my eldest daughter had fetched the flyswatter from the closet.

"It's too risky," I told her as I watched the hornet fly around the kitchen at near supersonic speeds. Carefully and slowly I walked back into the kitchen, opened a small closet door and reached for a can of hornet spray which I had purchased the year before to annihilate a hive by the livingroom window.

As I removed the cap, I suddenly felt like Lucas McCain, the famed *Rifleman* on TV. It was one of my favorite TV shows when I was growing up. In fact, I once got a toy *Rifleman* rifle for my birthday. I had forgotten about the *Rifleman* until recently when by accident I discovered it being aired on one of the cable TV stations. There was Lucas and that weird looking rifle going up against some bad guy after little Mark.

And there I was with my can of hornet spray going up against a bad guy threatening my children.

The hornet was obviously upset. A mad hornet is a flying hornet; a happy hornet is a hornet at rest. This particular hornet refused to land, so I knew he was mad.

I also knew I'd have but one shot. If I missed, he'd likely come right at me or at one of the girls. I don't care what anyone says, a hornet knows who's trying to do him in.

Suddenly the hornet flew past me, coming within inches of my face. Yes, he knew I was after him.

As my youngest girl clung to my pants leg, I raised the can to my chest, gave it a couple of hard shakes and pointed it in the general direction of the hornet.

"Come on you lousy hornet, land," I mumbled to myself. I knew if he did land, it would only be for a second or two.

"Look daddy!" The 5-year-old cried out.

Sure enough the hornet had landed, landed right on a can of Mountain Dew I had just opened. I had a clear shot, but to fire would mean sacrificing an entire can of soda. I decided to wait for another opportunity.

The hornet eventually flew off and resumed its circular flight pattern around the kitchen.

Suddenly it landed on the microwave about six feet away from me. It was just a few inches below a collection of houseplants. It was a long, risky shot. If I missed, I'd not only have a hornet after me, but my wife would probably kill me for killing one or more of her plants with the toxic spray.

Like Lucas McCain taking aim with his rife, I quickly raised my can and pressed the button. A clear stream of liquid shot out from the can, arced across the room and slammed right into the back of the hornet. Instantly the bug dropped dead to the floor.

Ol' Lucas couldn't have shot better. I blew across the spray nozzle as if it were a smoking barrel, capped it and put the can on the counter.

I bent down on one knee, grabbed my two girls and gave them a big hug. "It's over," I said softly as I heard the theme to the *Rifleman* playing in my mind.

142

Cartoons lead to conflict

My kids have given me a bad habit.

It is a habit I thought I had broken when I left home for college.

My kids have me watching afternoon cartoon shows.

It's terrible and I feel really guilty. I don't know if other parents succumb to this; I'm afraid to ask them.

It all happened very insidiously.

I'd come home from work and find the kids watching cartoons. At first I didn't pay any attention. I sorted through the day's mail, went to the bedroom to change into casual clothes and then helped my wife in the kitchen (the amount of help I offered is subject to debate).

One day, I came home particularly tired. In fact, I was beat. Writing is hard work. Don't let anyone fool you, pounding the keys of a PC is exhausting.

Anyway, I came home dead tired and plopped down on the couch. Not having the energy to read, I sat and watched *GI Joe* on the tube.

Not bad, I said to myself.

I felt relaxed, almost on the verge of napping.

Ghostbusters came on.

"Hey, this isn't bad. Those weird ghosts and goblins remind me of some of the people I work with," I muttered to myself.

I would have watched *The Flintstones*, but my wife came in, dragged me off the couch and pushed me to the supper table.

"Gee, honey, you know they are still running *Flintstone* cartoons on TV. Why I remember watching them as a kid. They were unusual because they were shown in prime time."

"Yes, dear," my wife said with a long sigh.

The following day when I came home from work, the kids were watching a show called *COPS*.

"What's this?" I asked my 5-year-old.

"A cartoon."

"Never seen this one before," I said sitting down in my easy chair.

For some strange reason I felt drawn to the animation of this particular cartoon show. It presented a futuristic city with hip, highly stylized characters. It was sort of a *GI Joe* does *Police Story*. Before I knew it, I was hooked. That afternoon I watched the entire episode.

The following day, I found myself rushing home from the bus so that I wouldn't miss that day's episode of*COPS*.

At first I tried to rationalized my watching cartoons. It's a legitimate art form, I told myself. As long as I only watch one a day, I'll be all right. I mean, it could be worse. I could come home every night and down a scotch and water.

My wife didn't seem to mind my cartoon watching.

So long as I was in the livingroom watching TV, the kids were in the livingroom out of her hair. In fact, I think subconsciously she encouraged me to watch the cartoons. I began to notice supper was being served later and later as my wife enjoyed her new found freedom more and more.

The only time she really minded was when one of her friends paid a visit. She didn't want other wives in the neighborhood to see her husband watching the *Road Runner*. She feared the neighbors might think her husband a bit loony tunes.

Things went along all right until one day one of the networks changed its programming schedule. The change pitted *Lassie* reruns against *COPS*.

"Can daddy watch *COPS*?" I politely asked my eldest daughter.

"I want *Lassie*," she snapped back as she pushed my hand away from the TV's tuner knob.

"But daddy has worked hard all day to provide food, shelter, clothing and, most importantly, toys for you and your sister. Don't you think he deserves to watch just one, itty bitty cartoon?"

144

"I don't like *COPS!*" she said indignantly.

"You did before."

That was a dumb thing to say. Early in my parenting career, I learned that if my daughters liked something one day, it was no guarantee they'd like it the next day. For instance, they love peas on Monday, hate them on Tuesday and two weeks later they love them again.

"Tell you what. If you let me watch *COPS*, I'll let you watch *The Flintstones*," I bargained. Since *The Flintstones* ran opposite the evening news, I thought my offer was more than generous.

My daughter just glared at me as she stood protecting the tuner knob.

"How about a cookie?"

"DONALD!" My wife yelled from the kitchen. In her mind, to offer a cookie just prior to supper is a cardinal sin against parenthood.

"Well, she won't let me watch TV."

"Donald, come in here and help me with the salad," my wife replied, her tone showing some frustration.

My daughter watched my every move as I got up out of my easy chair and went into the kitchen. She figured I was engaged in some ploy to get at the tuner.

I guess in retrospect I should be thankful for *Lassie* and my daughter's stubbornness. After a few days of anguish, I managed to break my habit of watching *COPS*. Peace came once more to the Oakland household.

I just have one problem now. I have this compulsion to watch *The Flintstones* instead of the evening news.

DRIVING DON CRAZY CHRONICLES

Parents plagued by potty paranoia

Small children don't realize the power they have.

Why with four little words, they can bring parents— any adult in fact— to their knees in an instant.

"I gotta go potty."

Any adult within earshot will instantly stop what he or she is doing and rush over to the kid. They will risk life and limb to whisk that child to the nearest restroom.

I remember once when my 3-year-old was with me in a crowded discount store when she suddenly she stopped, yanked on my pants leg and announced. "Daddy, I've got to go potty."

I scooped her up and tucked her under my arm like a fumbled football and took off down the aisle dodging women and shopping carts like a Chicago Bears halfback seeing daylight. I tore through the home furnishings, nearly knocking over a display of lightbulbs. I cut through the automotive section, pushing a rather burly fellow into a display of sparkplugs. I leaped over a display of plastic wastepaper baskets, brushed past potted plants and roared into the restroom... the women's restroom.

I don't know which was louder, the screams of women or the squeal of my tennis shoes as I skidded into an impromptu pirouette and ran out the door to seek refuge in the men's room.

Kids don't understand the meaning of holding it.

I used to say to them, "Can't you wait until we get home?" Many soggy pants later, I gave up asking. A kid's concept of time is here and now... 30 seconds into the future is too long to wait.

Adults don't have that luxury.

My life has been spent "holding it."

When I was in college, I had to "hold it" while I finished semester examinations.

I have had to "hold it" on trips because of misjudgments of the distance between gasoline stations.

When I was a reporter, I had to "hold it" many times. I mean, you can't stand up in the middle of a City Council meeting and say "Excuse me gentlemen, could you postpone that vote until I go potty?"

Covering after dinner speeches were real killers. During the meal, I'd drink a lot of coffee so that I would stay awake to hear the speaker. And it worked. I stayed awake through the dullest of speeches... not because of the caffeine, but because of the pain emanating from my bladder.

I have stood at parties with my knees together and turning blue in the face while I listened to someone tell me about the joys of their life. You can't just interrupt a person in mid sentence and dash off to the biff. Making matters worse, when I drink beer, I don't get much warning. Beer lets go all at once. There is no gradual feeling of filling up. It shoots from empty to bladder bursting in a matter of seconds.

148

Actually, I'm glad my body is accustomed to "holding it." You see, in the Oakland household, we have only one bathroom. And unfortunately, my daughters have priority access.

Like I'll get a feeling of fullness, so to speak, and start heading for the bathroom.

The instant my 3-year-old spots me walking toward the bathroom, she immediately announces she, too, has to go potty.

"Daddy has to go first," I tell her gently.

"I gotta go real bad," she pleads.

"All right get in there."

She runs into the bathroom and shuts the door.

Minutes pass. I'm clawing the walls in pain.

"Are you done yet?"

No answer.

My insides feel like a pressure cooker.

"Hurry dear."

No answer.

Five minutes pass. My internal fuse has been lit. If I don't get to a toilet in two minutes, it will be like a pin hitting a water balloon.

Normally I respect my children's privacy, but this is an emergency. I push open the door.

There is my daughter waist deep in toilet paper.

"I thought you had to go potty?"

She just smiles up at me and yanks another six yards of toilet paper off the roll.

I scoop her up and gently put her outside the door. I slam the door shut and seek relief.

My daughter begins banging on the door.

"I'm just about done," I shout as I flush the toilet and head for the door. Just as I step out the door, the toilet makes a funny sound.

"Oh, Lordy!"

When I flushed the toilet I had neglected to notice that the leading end of the toilet paper my daughter had unraveled was resting in the bowl. As the water began to flush away, it pulled the toilet paper off the floor and over the edge of the toilet bowl like the uncoiling of line attached to an anchor.

The toilet groans, gurgles and grinds to a complete halt. Then the flow of water reverses and starts quickly rising to the top of the bowl. Before I can get underneath the lid, water has spilled over and has turned the pile of toilet paper on the floor into a soggy pink mess.

Just then the 5-year-old comes running up to the bathroom door.

"Dad, I got to go to the bathroom real bad."

A dad's ticket to traction

I should teach a class called "Dumb Things Dads Do."

With my experience, I could save a lot of fathers a lot of grief.

I thought about this class the other day as I soaked in a tub of hot water, a last ditch attempt to stop a muscle spasm in my back.

I would call my first class: " Snowmen: Your Wintertime Ticket to Traction."

Every winter, Wisconsin gets snow. Before I became a dad, I thought the worst part of winter was shoveling snow. Shoveling was always good for at least one pulled muscle. And I hated getting out of bed an hour early, putting a coat over my pajamas and spending the next half hour removing snow from the drive-way and walk.

But shoveling is nothing in comparison to the pain and suffering a snowman can inflict on an unsuspecting dad.

My story begins with a thaw we had early in December. The first drops of snow melting off the roof sent my daughters screaming into our bedroom one morning: "Daddy let's make a snowman!"

"A Frosty the Snowman!" my 3-year-old exclaimed as she pulled the covers off me.

I walked out into the livingroom, opened the drapes and looked out at the blanket of snow covering our front lawn.

"I don't know if it's warm enough," I replied. Just then the paperboy spotted my eldest daughter in the livingroom window and chucked a snowball at her.

"Yup, it's warm enough," I sighed as I watched the mass of snow slide down the window.

Actually I was enthusiastic about the chance to make a snowman. It was something that I could do with both girls. It was something we could share in creating. My wife was also enthused. She gets excited anytime I can get both kids out of the house.

Later that morning, I was out in the wet snow with my two girls. "You know how you build a snowman?" I asked the 3-year-old. She shook her head.

I walked across the front lawn, bent down and fashioned a clump of snow between my gloves. Then I put it on the ground and began rolling it back and forth across the yard.

"See how easy it is," I said.

I could tell she wasn't impressed. She just sat in the snow and chewed on a clump of the white stuff.

My 5-year-old wasn't impressed either. She pointed at a snowman three doors down the street. Then she looked at the snowball I had rolled. "Daddy, can you build a snowman as big as that one."

"Sure, no problem," I said looking at my snowball, which seemed about half the diameter of the base of the snowman up the block.

Back and forth I went until the ball grew so big and so heavy I could no longer roll it with my arms. I had to put my shoulder into it and push with both legs, a real trick on a snow covered lawn. Finally I could push no more. "Well, I guess this is the best spot for our snowman," I told my girls. So what if half of it was on the sidewalk.

I glanced at the snowman up the street and determined that my bottom was bigger.

"OK girls, let's get the body built!"

My eldest daughter had already started the snowball rolling. My youngest still sat chewing on a clump of snow, still unimpressed by the wonderful winter sculpture being assembled.

Back and forth my daughter and I went until we had a ball of snow more than two feet in diameter. I rolled it next to the base of the snowman.

"Now I'll just lift this onto the base and then we'll start making the head," I told the 5-year-old as I dug my gloved hands into the tightly rolled ball of snow.

It didn't budge.

I changed position slightly so that I was lifting more with my legs.

"AAAAAAAAAAAGH!" I yelled like a Russian weightlifter. I could feel the snowball moving, but I could also feel muscles in my back and shoulders shaking and my knees starting to cave in.

Suddenly my grip slipped and the mass of snow came crashing down on my feet. "YEEEEEOOOW!"

I had hoped the impact would have split the snowball in half, but unfortunately it stayed intact.

"Are you all right?" My eldest daughter asked.

"I'm fine, dear. It's just the ball of snow is a tad bit heavier than I expected."

I saw her glance at the snowman up the street.

"But it's nothing daddy can't handle," I said trying to reassure her and preserve my ego.

I sat down in the snow and stared at the two balls of snow.

Who am I trying to kid, I thought to myself. There's no way I'm going to get that ball of snow up there. Heck, the heaviest thing I lift in a day is a ream of paper. I'm a writer not a weightlifter.

"Daddy, hurry! The snow is starting to melt," my eldest daughter said.

I got up and once again tried to lift the snowman's body. Once again it didn't move.

Suddenly I was saved by inspiration.

I rushed into the garage and reappeared a few minutes later with a long two by four. I laid one end against the base of the snowman thereby creating a ramp on which to roll the body into position.

I rolled the big ball to the foot of the ramp and then took a few deep breaths. "AAAAARGH!" I yelled as I put all my strength behind that ball. Up the ramp it slid. "It's working, it's working!" I cried out.

Suddenly my boots slipped. The next thing I knew I was face down in the snow with that big ball of white stuff sitting square on the middle of my back.

"You all right, daddy?" My eldest daughter asked as she tried to roll the big snowball off my back.

I turned and the big ball of snow rolled off. "Stand back, I'm mad now."

My daughter gave me an odd look and then took a few steps back. I whipped around and charged at that big ball like a Packer on a blitz. My shoulder slammed into the packed snow and pushed that ball of snow right up the ramp and over the top of the base.

There I laid, my stomach draped over the base of the snowman and my face embedded in the other ball of snow.

Once again I got up, rolled the snowball to the foot of the ramp and pushed. I pushed so hard it felt like trying to free a Buick stuck in a snowbank. Up it went and after what seemed like many minutes of excruciating effort, the big snowball was finally atop the base of the snowman.

I thought that would have warranted a cheer from my daughters. But they hardly noticed. My 3-year-old was still eating snow; the other girl was starting on the head of the snowman.

"Why don't we call it quits," I said to my eldest daughter. "How about we just have a dwarf snowman."

She shook her head.

"OK, but just realize our snowman is going to have a small head."

When the ball of snow reached roughly the diameter of a basketball, I grabbed it away from my daughter. I thought it was of sufficient size for a head.

Figuring that lifting it would be a piece of cake, I bent down and picked it up with a quick jerk. Suddenly every muscle in my lower back called it quits.

I managed to slip the head onto the snowman's shoulders just before my body collapsed into a heap on the snow. My wife came rushing out of the house as my daughters whipped snowballs at my curled up body.

Slowly she got me to my feet and helped me into the house. I groaned and cried as my wife pulled off my jacket. As she left to draw me a hot bath, I looked out the window at my marvelous snowman. I watched as my eldest daughter climbed up the two by four ramp.

"Honey!" I cried out to my wife. "Get outside quick before it's too late."

As my wife came running into the livingroom, I watched as my daughter climbed up the side of the snowman until she was perched on top of its head.

"Look at me, daddy!" She yelled.

Suddenly the shoulders of the snowman gave way and I watched as the whole creation came tumbling down. My daughter landed on top of the big mound of snow that was a few seconds before a magnificent man of snow.

Had I not been in so much pain, I would have thrown myself into a snowbank.

Tyke on a bike is trying

I wonder if birds teaching their young to fly is as rough as what parents go through trying to teach their children how to ride a bike?

Having just gone through the experience, I think I'd rather be a flight instructor for a robin. Flying has got to be easier to learn than steering a two wheel bicycle for the first time.

Last summer we got our eldest daughter a two-wheel bicycle with training wheels and it took her no time to learn how to pedal it around the neighborhood, much to the dismay of anyone who chose to walk down our sidewalks.

However, learning to turn was a different story. After a couple of spills, she soon learned that training wheels aren't made for high speed power turns.

At the end of the summer, I figured she was ready for the big step to two wheel travel.

"OK, all you have to do is pedal hard and steer straight. Got that?" I asked softly. She nodded.

Off we went. I held the bike upright with one hand on the seat as I ran along side.

"Pedal!" I yelled. "Pedal as hard as you can!"

And she did. She stomped down on the pedals so hard the bike lurched out of my hand and shot down the sidewalk.

"Steer! Steer!" I screamed as the bike wove from one side of the sidewalk to the other. Suddenly I realized that being able to steer a bike with training wheels, doesn't necessarily mean you can steer a bike without them.

The bike careened off the sidewalk, dug deep ruts into my neighbor's freshly watered front lawn and slammed into one of those shiny globe lawn ornaments like a Number 1 wood whacking a golf ball off a tee. I can't remember who was crying more that afternoon, my daughter, my neighbor or me.

"You dummy!" a co-worker told me after I related this sad

story. "You don't teach a kid how to ride a bike on a sidewalk. You take the kid to a large, flat parking lot when it's free of cars. She won't have to worry about steering there."

Taking his advice, my wife and I took our two daughters to a shopping center parking lot one Sunday afternoon. I put my 5-year-old on her bike and let the 3-year-old watch and wander around the vacant lot.

Although she was a little wobbly at first, my daughter soon was pedaling like a pro. As I watched her, I was filled with exhilaration and pride having just given my daughter her first step toward freedom... training wheels to two wheels, two wheels to tenspeeds, tenspeeds to "Hey dad can I borrow the car keys, please."

This moment of sublime self satisfaction abruptly ended when my wife screamed, "Donald! Stop her! She's heading for her sister!"

I looked up and saw my prodigious pedaler closing in on the unsuspecting 3-year-old. It was at that instant I remembered that I had neglected to teach my daughter the finer points of bicycling, such as respect for pedestrians and how to brake.

Fortunately I also forgot to teach her how to steer. Her bike wobbled and seemingly on its own volition veered away from the little tyke, who thought the near miss was great fun.

I was just about to return to my feeling of sublime self satisfaction when I saw the bike make an unexpectedly sharp turn and position itself perpendicular to our van. Like a kamikaze pilot, my daughter brought that bike right into the side of the vehicle. Neither my daughter nor her bike suffered a scratch. I wish I could have said the same for my van.

All I can say is it is a good thing birds don't ride bikes and kids can't fly.

Kids make dad pay when he leaves for the Wildwoods

Kids make you pay for your vacations.

Take them along and you'll pay for disrupting their lives. They'll scream in the car; they'll not go to bed at night; they'll ruin meals at restaurants and visits to vacation spots.

I have found that even if you don't take the kids, they'll make you pay.

Every September I take a week off and go fishing in Canada. It is my escape from work, parenthood and all the other responsibilities of life.

My wife has become accustomed to my flight to Canada and doesn't object as strongly as she did when we were first married.

But my kids object.

In subtle and in not so subtle ways, they let me know that they don't particularly like my leaving. Take for instance, my last trip to the wilderness.

It was the night before I was to leave. I went to bed early because I knew the next day I'd be up all night making the 12-hour non-stop trip.

As I recall, it was about 2 a.m. when my youngest daughter started crying. Normally she would cry for a few minutes and then go back to sleep. But not this night. This night she wouldn't stop.

My wife got up and gave the kid a glass of water.

She continued crying.

My wife picked her up and rocked her.

She continued crying.

By this time, I was fully awake and out of bed.

I tried rocking her.

She continued crying.

I tried singing to her.

She continued crying louder than before.

I tried feeding her yogurt.

She ate it quietly, but after she had finished it she started crying again.

The crying succeeded in waking up her sister, who normally sleeps through anything. She came into the livingroom in a lousy mood and commenced to cry.

I think it was 4 a.m. before we were able to get both kids back to bed.

An hour later, my youngest daughter started crying again.

Something was amiss for sure.

We got up and took her temperature. Sure enough she had a slight fever. My wife suggested I take her into the doctor's office later that morning.

I was assigned the job because I had decided to take the day off work so that I could get organized and be well rested before the long trip to Canada.

Instead of packing my gear, I found myself sitting in a doctor's waiting room.

Because my daughter didn't have the good sense to announce a day ahead of time that she was getting sick, we had to take what they call a "walk-in appointment." That means, they try to squeeze you in between all those lucky people who had appointments.

Normally we would be in and out of the doctor's office in a half hour, 45 minutes max. But this day, that amount of time had passed and we had yet to get beyond the waiting room door.

My daughter didn't mind. She was having a great time pulling magazines off tables, scattering toys around the room and wandering into the business office. Every time I'd start to read a magazine article, I'd have to get up and chase after the kid.

I was beginning to get a headache.

The kid was beginning to get hungry and ornery.

An hour had passed.

The kid was climbing a bookcase.

I pulled the kid off the bookcase and put her on the floor.

She charged right back to the bookcase and started climbing, this time nearly putting one foot through the top of an aquarium sitting on a lower shelf.

I yanked the kid off the bookcase once again.

She didn't like it a bit and proceeded to throw a temper tantrum right in the middle of the waiting room.

My headache was getting worse.

"Come on darling, don't you know dad needs to relax. He's got a long trip tonight," I pleaded.

She continued crying.

The commotion must have encouraged the doctor to find time for us because the nurse suddenly appeared and called us in.

I thought my troubles were over.

And my daughter had stopped crying.

It would be a few minutes and then the doctor would come in, make his diagnosis and we'd be out of here. I'd still have time to organize my gear and take a late afternoon nap, I thought to myself.

That would have occurred had it not been the day before my vacation. Instead of seeing the doctor right away, we waited another 20 minutes in the exam room.

If you ever want a tension headache quickly, just lock yourself in a 10 by 10 foot exam room with a 3-year-old. Nothing was safe.

She ripped the paper off the examination bench.

She squirted some antiseptic liquid soap all over the walls.

She knocked over a container of tongue depressors.

She pooped in her diaper. It wasn't a normal poop. It was a runny, messy poop. The odor– concentrated by the smallness of the room– nearly made ME sick.

Finally the doctor came in. After a few questions, he decided to examine her ears, something which the 3-year-old hates with a passion. I grabbed her and as she screamed into my ears, the doctor looked quickly into her ears.

"I think she has an ear infection," the doctor said.

Or at least that's what I think he said. All I could hear was a ringing in my ears.

Finally it was over. The diagnosis was made; the medicine was ordered, and we were on our way home. I figured I would have just enough time to throw my gear into the car and go.

Had I not been going on vacation that night, that's what would have happened.

Instead I got home only to find that while I was gone, our 5-year-old had gotten into my backpack and had scattered the contents all over the livingroom.

Parents pay when they take a vacation.

Lottery's lesson: Gambling to guilt

I bought my first Wisconsin Lottery ticket the other day.

Actually I bought five. Someone had told me that if you only buy one, you won't win anything. People who win the big prizes buy ten or twenty dollars worth at a crack.

All I had in my wallet was a $10 bill and I had promised to buy my girls ice cream cones. I bought five tickets and three ice cream cones. I grabbed the cones in one hand and the tickets in the other and ran out to the van to check my numbers.

I felt lucky that morning.

Even when one of the ice cream cones slipped from my fingers and smeared against the tickets my optimism wasn't dampened. However, I did have a passing thought about the state not accepting sticky tickets. Can you imagine sending in a $5,000 winning ticket and have it returned with this terse message: "State law 555.41 (c) provides that redeemed lottery tickets must be in good condition so as to be processed by our computers. Your ticket stuck to the transport rollers of the computer. We are sorry but your ticket is too sticky to be acceptable. Please play again and have a good day."

I wiped off the tickets with a dirty tissue. I figured the state wouldn't notice the remnants of a sneeze smeared on their shiny tickets.

Taking my thumbnail, I scratched the covering off the first number.

$5000.

"Good lord! We're going to be rich!" I shouted.

The girls gave me a puzzled look and continued eating their ice cream cones. I was so excited I didn't notice that the 3-year-old had allowed her chocolate-covered vanilla cone to drop onto the seat.

I took a deep breath and scratched until another number was revealed.

$50,000

"Let's see, first thing I'm going to do is sign up for a Caribbean cruise, just me and the wife. When I get home, I'm going to buy the best stereo system and dozens of CDs," I said to myself. Then feeling a tinge of guilt, I added... "And the rest I'll put in a savings account for the girls' college education."

I hurriedly scratched another number into view.

$5.

I needed that, a breather from the tension.

I slowly scratched the next number.

$50,000.

I knew it! Why I could put the amount into stocks, go part time on my job and write books the rest of the time, I thought to myself.

"Hey, how'd you like daddy home with you all the time," I yelled back to the kids.

The 5-year-old looked up. "Dad, can I have another ice cream cone?"

"Yeah, maybe you're right, daddy shouldn't be home all

day... you'd drive him crazy and mommy would end up killing him," I said ignoring her request.

The 3-year-old picked up her cone from the seat, smiled and then proceeded to shove the half melted cone into the left cheek of her sister. Suddenly the van was filled with screams and crying.

"Settle down girls, your daddy is about to become rich," I said trying to ignore the civil war in the backseat.

I rubbed another number.

$5

I began sweating.

Ever so slowly I scraped the covering off the sixth number. $1.

"AAAAAAUGH!"

My anguished cry shocked the kids so much they momentarily stopped fighting.

I took a deep breath and ripped off the second ticket.

"Be bold," I said to myself and then scratched the entire ticket within a few seconds.

Zilch.

I ripped off the third ticket.

The closest thing I came to winning was $5.

On the fourth ticket, I scratched it number by number. My spirits rose for a moment when I scratched into view $100,000. Unfortunately nothing matched. I picked up the last ticket.

"OK, OK, I've paid my dues. Just think positively. I have to picture in my mind the winning numbers. Yes, I see $50,000 in my mind. Do it!" I said confidently.

I ripped through the card with my thumbnail: $5000, $50, $50, $10, Entry and Entry.

"AAAAAAAUGH!"

"Why did I do it? Why did I throw $5 away? I could have bought a 12-pack of premium beer for that. I could have bought the best steak in the store for that," I moaned.

The 5-year-old sat quietly watching me. She wasn't quite sure what her daddy was up to and figured it must be something she had done. The 3-year-old was oblivious to it all as she sat playing in the puddle of vanilla and chocolate ice cream on the upholstery.

"Don't tell mommy what I've done," I told the 5-year-old.

"OK, daddy," she said.

As I drove home, I thought about all the things I could have done with that $5. I thought about my father-in-law who recently had turned in a $10 winning ticket. I thought about the secretary at work who had turned in a $5 ticket, used it to purchase five more tickets, one of which yielded $50.

I thought about how the furnace had gone out the night before and the $60 repair bill. I thought about my VISA bill which had ballooned into a monster because of an overly generous Christmas.

As we pulled into the driveway, I vowed never again to play the lottery, not unless I found a $10 bill on the curb or came into an inheritance.

The 5-year-old jumped out of the car and rushed into the house. As I walked in the front door, I could hear her tell mommy about the ice cream cones, about how her sister had spilled her cone on the seat and how daddy was playing with these funny looking tickets and talking to himself.

Kids turn off to turn on

Where do kids get all that energy?

Parents ask themselves that question often, usually at night when they finally have put the kids to bed and have collapsed totally exhausted onto the couch. They have barely enough energy left to turn on the TV with the remote control.

There are a number of theories addressing that question.

One favorite is the vampire hypothesis. Parents who subscribe to this theory believe that small children psychically suck energy from their parents much like vampires suck blood from their victims.

The more energy parents have, the wilder the kids are simply because the kids have a deeper reservoir to draw from.

Another theory holds that because children are smaller than their parents, the effects of gravity are less. Therefore, children can be more active without expending a lot of energy resisting the gravitational pull of the Earth.

I offer one further theory. I call it the light switch syndrome.

My contention is children are experts in energy conservation. It is an instinctive skill rather something learned.

Small children simply shut down.

Here's a case in point.

A while back, we took our two children to Mill Bluff State Park near Tomah, Wisconsin, for a weekend of camping. The attraction of this park is the bluffs and the view they offer.

One afternoon, my wife and I told the girls we would take them to the top of one of the bluffs. The kids were excited. They didn't know a bluff from a buffalo, but they did know what climbing meant. And they love to climb.

"How are we going to get up there?" my wife asked as she gazed up at a towering bluff.

"Easy, we just follow this path which leads to a stairway that goes all the way to the top," I said looking at the park brochure.

The two girls took off running.

"Better go after them. I don't want them climbing those stairs alone," my wife said.

I took off running. I quickly caught up to the 3-year-old and scooped her up into my arms. The 5-year-old I met at the bottom of the stairs.

"Daddy, I'm tired," the 5-year-old announced.

"What?"

"I'm tired."

"It's 10 o'clock in the morning, how can you be tired? Just two minutes ago you were racing around like an Olympic sprinter." I put down the 3-year-old. The instant her feet touched the ground she began crying.

"What's the matter with you?"

"Carry me, daddy."

"And me, too," the 5-year-old said quickly.

Just then my wife walked up.

"Dear, the kids are too tired to walk up the stairs. They want me to carry them up. Can you take one?"

My wife shook her head. She was lugging a small cooler full of pop and sandwiches at the time.

"Come on kids, you can walk up these stairs. Heck, at grandpa's house, you run up and down his stairs 50 times a day."

The 3-year-old resumed crying.

The 5-year-old sat down on a step and refused to budge.

"OK! You win." I lifted the two girls into my arms and started up the stairs.

Fifty steps up I thought I was going to die of a heart attack. My arm muscles were locking up and my pulse was racing. In addition, the 3-year-old had yanked off my glasses, and the 5-year-old was kicking me in the leg and shifting her weight from side to side.

"You can walk the rest of the way," I pleaded.

"I'm too tired, daddy," my eldest daughter replied.

"I'm tired, too," the 3-year-old mimicked.

Somehow I made it up what seemed like a mile of stairs. When I reached the top, I let down the kids and grabbed for the stair railing for support. I pulled myself up to a bench and fell onto it.

I looked up and the kids were racing around, running from one end of the bluff to the other and back again.

My wife joined me on the bench. She found me soaked in sweat and trying to catch my breath. After about 10 minutes rest, I summoned enough strength to get off the bench and go look at the view. I felt like I was 80.

I couldn't even take pictures. Every time I put the camera up to my eyes, my glasses would steam up from perspiration coming off my forehead.

"Time to go kids," I said wearily.

The two kids shot past me and headed down the stairs. The 3-year-old got three steps down before she stopped and sat down. The 5-year-old was halfway down before she stopped.

"What's wrong?" I asked the 3-year-old.

"I'm tired, carry me," she demanded.

"You're not tired and I'm not going to carry you," I said and continued down the steps. I figured she'd follow me. But she didn't. She just sat there stubbornly.

"Come on!"

She didn't move.

"Please."

She didn't move.

"I'm leaving and mom's leaving," I said and walked down a few more steps.

She began crying.

At that point, I knew it was hopeless. I knew the world wouldn't let me leave a crying kid on the top of a bluff even though I knew she was bluffing.

Up I went.

Up into my arms she went.

Down we went, step by step.

By the time I reached number two daughter, who was still sitting on a step, the muscles in my right arm were going into gridlock again.

"Daddy, I'm tired," the 5-year-old sighed.

Before I could tell her that there was no way I could carry her and her sister down the stairs, she had jumped up and thrown herself onto my free arm.

Down I went, two girls in two arms, one step at a time.

Somehow I made it down without collapsing. I felt like I had just portaged a canoe up and down a half mile long hill.

The instant I put the girls down they ran off.

It was as if they switched on and off their energy resources while dad drained his like the battery in a car with the lights left on.

As I walked down that trail to our van, I felt exhausted. I felt ready for bed even though there was at least another 10 hours to the day.

This is not an isolated example.

My kids do this to me all the time.

The other day, I took them to the shopping mall. Ten minutes into our visit, the 3-year-old announced she was quote unquote tired. So as I chased the 5-year-old from store to store, I had to carry the 3-year-old, all 35 pounds of her.

I was so exhausted from shopping, I was ready to call for EMTs.

But when we got home, my 3-year-old all of a sudden flicked on her energy switch and tore around the house as if she was turbocharged.

I'm convinced that kids get all their energy from the skillful allocation of energy resources and the careful manipulation of their parents.

Ham salad solves leftovers problem

I think I have finally solved the leftovers problem.

Ever since my wife and I have had children, we have had a leftovers problem.

It is impossible to predict how much our daughters will eat during a particular meal.

There are times they acted so hungry prior to dinner you'd

swear they'd eat the tablecloth. Yet when they sat down, suddenly they lost their appetite. Then I got wise. They weren't hungry for supper; they were hungry for snacks.

I have on occasion prepared perfectly delightful dinners only to have them sit on the kids' plates untouched because sometime during the afternoon, the kids snuck a snack or conned my wife out of a cookie.

I tell you, one cookie anytime after 2:00 in the afternoon will kill a dinner for a kid under 5.

Then there is the competition de cuisine. Daughter number one wants a macaroni and cheese with her hot dog. Daughter number two wants the same even though she has no intention of eating the macaroni and cheese. Both daughters demand salad because mommy and daddy are having salads. Yet when given their salads, the kids suddenly develop allergy ala lettuce.

"Eat your salad," I say sternly.

"I don't like lettuce," the eldest daughter complains.

"I don't like lettuce, either," the 3-year-old mimics.

"Well, why did you ask for it?"

"I didn't want that much," the 5-year-old replies.

"You only have one leaf and a few shavings of carrot. It's not like I'm asking you to eat a chef's salad!" I respond with growing frustration in my voice.

"I want a cookie," the 3-year-old interjects. That's what I like about 3-year-olds, they come at you with comments right out of leftfield.

"Dear, you haven't touched one thing on your plate, this is no time to be discussing cookies. Clean your plate and you'll get a cookie."

"I want a cookie, now!"

"No!"

The kid starts crying which means that for the next few minutes there will be absolutely no chance of anything on her plate being eaten.

Meanwhile, the 5-year-old eats half her meat, half her

168

potato and a third of her veggies...the salad remaining untouched. Before I can get her to eat a little more, she is off her chair, out of the kitchen and out the front door to play with her friends.

The bottom line is that after every meal there are leftovers. The trouble is, there isn't enough left over to constitute another meal. And I have found through experience it doesn't pay to save anything less than a full serving. Half servings tend to be forgotten and over time find their way to the rear of the refrigerator, there to mutate into some new lifeform.

My solution to this parental problem is simple: Ham salad sandwiches.

After every meal, I take what the kids don't eat and throw it all into our Cuisinart. I flick on the switch and let the sharp blades reduce the foodstuffs to a fine pulp. Then I spoon out the pulp and put it into a plastic container filled with ham salad. Next I throw the whole mess back into the Cuisinart and let 'er chew it up for about three minutes.

The secret to this concoction of convenience is sweet pickle relish, lots of it. Pickle relish, onion and a healthy dose of green pepper effectively mask anything you care to add to the ham salad.

I don't care if it is pot roast or fillet mignon, boiled potatoes or spinach dip— you put it in my ham salad, you'll never taste it.

If you add enough ham and mayonnaise, you can effectively mask the color of whatever extras you add.

With some early attempts, I had some trouble with lumpiness. However, I have since found three to five minutes in the Cuisinart takes care of lumps, no matter how large.

Now it might not be the nicest looking ham salad ever to grace a slice of bread, but by golly it is among the healthiest. What other kind of sandwich spread boasts three kinds of meat, potatoes and mixed vegetables. Why it is a virtual smorgasbord in a sandwich.

As soon as I perfect my masking techniques to a fine science, then I'll spring one of my sandwiches on the kids.

Call it sweet revenge.

Parents: Learn to powerlift

I have some advice for young men contemplating marriage. Start lifting weights.

You might think that I am making this suggestion so that these young men can hone their bodies into sexy hulks, thereby attracting the girls of their dreams.

On the contrary, this is a suggestion for survival, survival as a dad.

My children are destroying my body.

Had I pumped iron in my youth, this destruction may have been at best prevented, at the very least postponed.

One of the things they don't tell you about parenthood is the physical abuse you and your wife will endure picking up and carrying your children around.

It's not something that occurs to you early in parenthood. I mean, babies are nearly weightless. Unfortunately these feather-light creatures grow into two-ton toddlers.

Come on, you say, two-tons?

I'm not kidding.

My eldest daughter weighs in close to 50 pounds. I pick her up at least 10 times a day... a hug when I get home from work, lifting her off the top of the sofa, lifting her off the top of the livingroom table, lifting her onto her seat at the dinner table, lifting her back onto her seat after she jumps off to go harass her sister, lifting her to get a book off the shelf, lifting her in and out of the bathtub...

You add that all up, that's 500 pounds of lifting a day. Multiply that by seven days and you come darn close to 4000 pounds.

Considering the amount of physical exercise I get at work consists of punching the keys of a computer, the physical demands of raising kids is significant.

And it's starting to take its toll.

The other day I went to the doctor's office seeking help for a chronically sore left shoulder.

"Do any weightlifting or other strenuous exercise?" The doctor asked.

"Are you kidding. With two kids I don't have the time to exercise. My barbell set is buried under a mountain of spider webs in the basement. I have a Jane Fonda workout tape, but I find instead of watching it, I usually end up on the couch watching *Miami Vice* reruns with a beer in my hand."

"Are you a weekend athlete?"

"Nope, gave that up years ago after I decided one day to join my fellow workers in a game of flag football. By halftime I was benched with a bad back and a twisted ankle. My few moments of glory on the field, cost me plenty in physician and physical therapy fees."

"Do you roughhouse with your children?" He asked.

"Occasionally."

"And in playing with them, do you ever pick them up?"

"Sure."

The good doctor proceeded to explain there is little difference picking up a 50 pound barbell and a 40 pound girl. Without proper warm up and conditioning, one is bound, in either situation, to over stress muscles. "Particularly at your age," he laughed.

Then he prescribed some pills to ease the inflammation and suggested I begin a rather basic weightlifing program to improve my upper body strength.

"It's going to get worse, you know," he continued. "Little girls don't stay little for long."

"What are you saying?"

"I'm saying your kid could put you in the hospital if you're not careful."

"Comeon," I said shaking my head.

"Picture this... you're in a shopping mall with your two daughters. Suddenly your eldest daughter decides she is too tired to walk. Being a good dad, you bend over to pick her up. But instead of lifting with your knees like you are supposed to, you lift with your back...

"Rrrripp goes every muscle in your lower back. Your body curls like a dandelion in water and you fall to the floor, your body in a tight fetal position. People gather round as your daughter uses your body as an impromptu pillow to bounce upon. The EMTs come and pick up your body, which still resembles an overgrown pretzel.

"Three weeks of intense physical therapy and you're a daddy again," the doctor said as he walked me out the door.

So let this be a warning to you parents-to-be, before you start raising kids, you had better start raising weights.

Playroom becomes war room

In the Oakland household, we don't have a playroom. We have a war room.

This unusual room in our home is the product of one of those brilliant ideas parents have for attempting to corral the limitless energy of the under six set.

One day after our two kids had demolished our livingroom in two and a half minutes flat, we decided that rather than allowing our children to use the livingroom as their own playground, we would create their own playroom.

We decided to convert the youngest daughter's bedroom into the playroom. Being the youngest, she had accumulated the least, therefore, the fewest number of things to move.

To accomplish this household urban renewal project required the acquisition of a high rise sleeping structure, otherwise known as a bunk bed.

Much to our surprise, the kids accepted the bunk bed without the usual crying and temper tantrums. Our eldest daughter quickly laid claim to the top bunk. She bounced on the mattress a bit and then explored new ways of climbing up to the bed. To this day, she rarely uses the ladder.

Our youngest daughter, who was 2 years old at the time, didn't mind the lower bunk. In fact, she found great sport in grabbing our eldest daughter's legs whenever she dangled them over the edge of the top bunk.

We felt pretty good about our decision.

The kids were happy together.

The livingroom was clean and orderly.

No longer were we straining our backs frantically picking toys, Crayons and paper up off the livingroom floor as friends or relatives approached the front door.

All the kids' toys were neatly stored in marked boxes on shelves in the playroom.

In addition we installed some cheap carpet remnant to give them a play area.

The electrical outlets were covered.

And a deadbolt lock was installed on the outside of the door.

Everything was ready.

We threw the kids inside, told them to have a good time and then closed the door and bolted it.

Then we retired to the kitchen for a relaxing cup of coffee.

The explosion came as I was pouring my first cup of coffee. The concussion caused my right hand to jerk slightly to the left, which in turn caused the coffee to cascade down upon my left hand, which in turn caused me to drop the cup...on my foot, my barefoot.. which caused me to lose my balance and topple onto the table... the coffee pot on the table then poured its contents onto my wife's lap.

I don't know which was worse at that moment. The crashing sounds coming from the playroom or my wife's screaming. I abandoned my wife and headed for the playroom.

Beyond the door was a sight that would have made the

strongest of parents shudder.

In the middle of the room were our two girls.

They were happy and unharmed. But where they were sitting was the only place you could see floor.

Around them was a ring of two hundred and one Duplos and a couple dozen small, wooden blocks. Beyond that was every toy and stuffed animal they owned.

I surmised the explosion was caused when my eldest daughter decided to try out climbing skills she had learned on the bunk bed by trying to scale the newly installed playroom shelves. She had apparently been successful in reaching the first shelf. However, when she put weight on the second shelf, it and the one below it gave way, sending her, a dozen stuffed animals, two puzzles, a box of blocks and various toys for the 2-year-old crashing to the floor.

An hour later we had the playroom picked up. We told our eldest daughter that her mountain climbing days were over and once again left the girls alone to play.

This time there was little if any noise coming from the playroom.

For the next hour, my wife and I enjoyed our new found freedom.

"Better go check on the girls," my wife said reluctantly.

"Do I have to?" I asked looking up from a magazine. "Do you realize this is the first time I have been able to read a magazine in my own livingroom without interruption, without one of our precious daughters diving through my magazine and landing right in my, uh, lap."

"Dear, they can't stay in there all day."

"Why not?"

"Donald!" She said indignantly.

"OK, OK."

I wasn't quite prepared for what was behind the playroom door this time. Had I remembered the first rule of parenting–never trust quiet children–I may have been ready for what my daughters had done.

During the short time they had been in their, they had quietly opened a cabinet containing all the games and puzzles they had accumulated in their short lifetimes. And they had quietly removed each game and each puzzle. And they had quietly opened each game and each puzzle and had scattered the contents to every corner of the room.

Then they had war.

They threw pieces of puzzles at one another.

They took game pieces and cards and flung them about with wild, but quiet abandonment.

It took my wife and me the rest of the afternoon to sort out the pieces and puzzles.

"Why do they have to make games with six billion and one cards?" I cried out as I found a Candyland card wedged up in the ceiling light.

Every time the kids use the playroom, chaos ensues.

They can't play with one toy at a time. They have to clean off the shelves first. They have to empty every box.

They don't play with their toys, they nest in them.

And like war, the chaos never stays confined. It spreads. Like little smugglers, the kids sneak their toys and games out of the playroom into the livingroom. If my wife and I don't play border patrol, much of what was once in the playroom will be in the livingroom.

Then instead of one room, we have two to clean.

Ya can't win.

Practicing organized confusion

I am the most organized disorganized person I know. If that seems a contradiction, it is. Yet it is true.

I have this complusion to be organized. A place for everything and everything in its place is my motto.

The trouble is in the Oakland household there are too many places and too many things.

And I have discovered that whatever organizational abilities I possess are quickly and effectively weakened by one other pervasive trait of mine: procrastination.

Organization doesn't work if you put off doing it.

I know that our table linen should go in box number 22 in the basement. Instead the linen rests underneath a pile of magazines in the livingroom, magazines which either should have been discarded or taken into the basement and put in the boxes marked "Old Magazines."

I simply procrastinate putting things in their places even though I'm great at creating places.

There are times when I work myself into an organizational frenzy and spend hours in the basement numbering boxes and putting things in boxes and recording what went into which box. And after I'm all done, I'll look with a sense of accomplishment at the stacks of boxes and the handwritten records bound neatly in a three ring binder.

All will be right with the world so long as I don't remove anything from any of the boxes.

As soon as something leaves a box, it is gone for good. It will never return to that box.

We'll use an item from one of the boxes, but when it comes to putting the item away, I'll put off doing it until the item disappears. Six months later, I'll find it and decide that it should be returned to the box. I'll go downstairs, find the index of boxes, identify which box the item should be returned to and take it to that box. Unfortunately, I will discover that particular box doesn't exist.

It doesn't exist because three months ago, I removed it from its shelf and never got around to returning it. It still exists, but it is located somewhere else in the basement. It is one of more than 120 boxes tucked away along the walls.

And should I be lucky enough to find the proper box, I will likely discover that what was supposed to have been in there isn't in there.

Instead of winter clothes, there are kids' toys.

Instead of socks there are old magazines.

Instead of nuts, bolts and screws there are pictures, slides and negatives.

I'm convinced a gremlin lives in our house, a little creature who lives to change numbers on boxes.

Actually, it's no gremlin; it's my wife.

My wife doesn't share my flair for organization.

To her, a box is a box. Numbers are meaningless.

For instance, in spring I'll put my winter clothes in boxes 23, 45 and 67. Come summer, she'll need a box to mail something, so she'll take the clothes out of boxes 23 and 45, and put them in a larger unnumbered box. Come fall, I'll find box 67 but not 23 or 45. Then I'll spend hours searching through the vast collection of unnumbered boxes for the contents of the missing boxes numbered 23 and 45.

There are also times when I play a unique guessing game with myself. I find myself almost psychoanalyzing my mind or playing Sherlock Holmes with my thought processes as the culprit.

Take for example, the case of the missing flashlight.

"Honey, do you know where our flashlight is?" I ask my wife.

"Isn't it in one of your boxes?" she replies.

"No. It was supposed to have been in box 111, but it wasn't there."

177

"Didn't you use it last week when the kids threw your car keys behind the refrigerator?"

"You're right. Now where would I have put it down?"

"I have no idea," my wife says.

"I would have put it in a place where I knew I would look for it," I say to myself. "Now if you're Don Oakland and you just spent the last 30 minutes trying to get your car keys out from behind the refrigerator, where would you have put the flashlight?

"You were probably rushed, so you wouldn't have taken it far.

"You would have probably put it on top of the refrigerator, but you couldn't have because the top of the refrigerator was covered with bags of potato chips, Girl Scout cookies and stale bread.

"You might have put it in the livingroom on the bookshelf, but you wouldn't have because you knew your wife would later move it.

"Must have put it on your bureau in the bedroom!"

I rush to the bedroom. There is a ton of stuff on the top of the bureau, but a flashlight is not one of the items.

For the rest of the afternoon, I search for the flashlight. My investigation concludes abruptly when my wife asks me to run down to the store for milk and eggs. I go to the hall closet and as I reach in to grab my coat, I see the flashlight on the shelf next to my hat.

Suddenly everything becomes clear. Suddenly I remember that after getting my car keys, I had to use the car. I went to the closet and realizing I still had my flashlight in hand, I placed it on the shelf figuring that when I returned and went to hang up my coat, I'd see the flashlight and return it to its proper place. But I never made it back to the closet because I threw my coat on the livingroom chair figuring that I'd hang it up later.

I tell you, being organized is a real pain in the posterior.

THAT'S LIFE CHRONICLES

A time to soak and slide

A while back, my wife won a weekend vacation at a luxury condominium. It was a luxury condo, she told me, because it had a hot tub.

I wasn't impressed. To me, luxury is a big screen, stereo VCR system, not a glorified bath tub.

"Isn't it gorgeous," my wife exclaimed as we entered the livingroom of the "luxury villa."

"Nice," I said as I collapsed onto the couch. "I wonder if there is any beer in the refrigerator."

Discovering that our hosts indeed had left us a six-pack, I became more optimistic that I would enjoy myself.

"OK, where's this hot tub," I said looking out the patio window.

"It's upstairs," my wife said.

"Upstairs? I thought they only put hot tubs on patios," I said as I climbed the stairs toward our bedroom.

"Hey, dear! You gotta see this. They put the hot tub right next to the bed. Can you believe it! The architect who designed this must have been on drugs."

"Donald, it's supposed to be like that. It's more romantic that way."

"What's romantic about putting a bath tub by your bed. Satin sheets are romantic; taking a bath isn't."

"You don't take a bath in it, you sit and soak while sipping champagne," my wife said as she went to greet our hosts at the front door.

Feeling a bit grimy from the drive, I decided I'd try it out. I put my beer next to the tub and turned on the water.

While it filled, I glanced at a brochure on the bed and noted a picture of a hot tub filled with bubble bath. Finding a box of bubble mix in the bathroom, I dumped its contents into the big tub.

I turned the whirlpool control to 20 minutes and slipped into the churning water. Within minutes the tub was filling with suds like a washing machine gone berserk.

As I tried to slap the bubbles back into the tub, I was unaware that a hose within the hot tub had ruptured causing a leak of massive proportions. It was a leak that produced a waterfall which streamed down from the ceiling onto our hosts who were changing clothes in their downstairs bedroom.

Ear deep in suds, I heard none of their screams or my wife's desperate banging on the bedroom door. All I remember, albeit vaguely, was a loud crack, not unlike the snap of a large tree about to fall.

Suddenly the water soaked floor joists gave way and the tub and I were dropping like a runaway elevator to the bedroom below. Our hosts watched in horror as the tub hit their bed, bounced three feet into the air and careened through a plate glass picture window.

I held onto the side of the tub with one hand and held my

can of beer in the other. The traveling tub hit a snowbank, and like a bobsled shot down an icy ravine, crashed through a wood fence and slid down the snow covered Number 1 fairway of the resort's golf course.

Using search lights, the police found me a short time later sitting in the still warm suds of my tub, which had come to rest in a sandtrap.

As other residents of the resort gathered round the tub, I was thankful for the exhuberance of the bubble bath, which by then had frozen into a translucent glaze protecting my privacy.

I felt no guilt over what had occurred. I mean, anyone crazy enough to put a bathtub next to a bed in a room on the second floor was just asking for trouble.

A mouse in the house is maddening

If the writing in this particular essay seems a bit off, it is because the writer is feeling a little paranoid today.

There's a mouse in the house.

Every winter when the air turns cold and the snow blanket becomes crusty, mice migrate into my home.

Why? I don't know.

To the best of my knowledge, our home is relatively critter proof. Rodents have to work to get inside. But to them it is worth it. We don't have any cats or other pets which would harass a little mouse. Our basement is a cluttered mess, a virtual condominium complex for a vacationing rodent.

I guess what bothers me about mice is that I never see them, but I get the feeling they are always watching me. Like when I go into the basement, I sense that they are lurking behind boxes of old clothes. I get the feeling that if I pick up that dusty old box of discarded magazines, I will find a colony of mice happily housekeeping among the pages.

The other thing I don't particularly like about mice is they never come alone. They are like an old college buddy who comes for an unexpected visit, his wife, three kids, two dogs and a cat in tow.

Should I be lucky enough to trap a mouse, it does little to ease my fears because I know the rest of his or her family is still sneaking about the basement. And there is nothing I can do to keep them there.

If they want to explore the upstairs, they can. While I'm sleeping, the whole family may trek across my covers like a Boy Scout Troop on a 5-mile hike. Later when I awaken and discover their little brown calling cards on the covers, I feel a sense of violation and helplessness.

Maybe it's an attitude problem.

I mean, would things be different if mice had the same status as, say, rabbits.

Rabbits seem more like free pets than intruders.

When I was growing up, my family used to put food out in the backyard and watch the rabbits come by. It was a real treat when my friends and I would stumble upon a nest of rabbits and cuddle the little babies.

I remember when I had a squirrel friend in Clintonville, Wisconsin. He lived in the trees across the street. I would go out on my back porch, make a squeaking sound and he would appear amongst the branches. He'd run down the tree, cross the street and run up my sidewalk until he was within a few feet of my feet. I would feed him peanuts, cereal or whatever else was close to appropriate squirrel food.

But the thought of doing that with a mouse is abhorrent. I cannot picture myself searching out a nest of mice and cuddling their young. I cannot picture myself sitting on the kitchen floor making weird sounds to attract a little mouse who has taken up residence in a box of old insulated t-shirts and wool socks.

Maybe I'm wrong. Maybe I should consider this intrusion an opportunity for my daughters to experience firsthand the wonders of nature.

"Guess what kids? There is a mouse in the house," I announce enthusiastically.

My daughters continue to watch cartoons on the TV.

"Aren't you excited? Turn off the TV and let's go looking for them."

My daughters give me a bewildered look and turn back to watching *Alf* on the tube.

I walk over and turn off the TV. "Get your shoes on, we're going down to the basement."

"Nooooo, not the basement. Dad I hate it down there. It's creepy and dirty and there are spiders and things with millions of legs and I get all scared and turn the TV back on...pleeeese," the 5-year-old begs.

"Nonsense. I'll get a piece of cheese and we'll see if we can coax him out from his hiding place. I'll get my camera and we'll take a picture of him. Maybe you and your sister can get close enough that I can get a picture of the three of you. Wouldn't that make a dandy Christmas card?"

"Daddy!" The 5-year-old says. "That's gross!"

The 3-year-old just smiles.

"See your sister thinks it is a good idea."

"Dad, she doesn't know what you're talking about," the 5-year-old replies.

"Sure she does."

The 5-year-old turns to her sister. "Mice eat little girls in the night!" The little one smiles.

"See."

"Heck, she knows you are just kidding. Mice might nest in the socks in your drawer, but they aren't interested in eating you," I tell the 3-year-old.

The 5-year-old looks startled.

"What do you mean nesting in my socks?"
"Forget I said anything," I say as I look for my camera.

"You mean they could be in MY DRAWERS!"
"Nah."
"Daddy!"
"Nothing could live in your room. It is such a mess," I say with a chuckle.
"Daddy!"
"Don't worry about it."
"Daddy, I'm afraid to get my clothes. I'll never get dressed again. I'll have to go to preschool in my pajamas."
The argument continues for another 15 minutes and tops the conversational agenda at supper. That night the kids have a hard time going to sleep because they have a mouse on their minds.
Mouse paranoia has been successfully passed down to another generation of the Oakland family.

Kim Basinger is in my bathroom

I've got a problem.
Kim Basinger is in my bathroom.
Every time I go into the bathroom, whether it be to brush my teeth or bathe, Ms. Basinger is there staring at me.
She's not actually there. She's on the cover of the magazine which is on the floor in front of the toilet.
You see, like many Americans, my wife and I have gotten into the habit of putting magazines in the bathroom. One of the magazines is the type which features profiles of celebrities. As a consequence, each week the magazine usually has a picture of

some movie or TV star on its front cover.

The current issue has a sexy looking Kim Basinger on the cover, a cover I see every time I enter the bathroom. Even though I've read the magazine, it has somehow avoided a trip to the trash can.

It's getting unnerving.

I get the feeling she is watching me as I stand naked next to the bathtub or as I step onto the scale. Her eyes never leave me.

It didn't bother me when Mel Gibson was on the cover or William Hurt.

But Ms. Bassinger certainly has me bothered in the bathroom.

It has reached the point where I'm starting to talk to her. I figure it is less crazy to talk to a starlet on a magazine cover than it is to talk to oneself in the mirror.

"What do you think, Kim?" I whisper as I stand on the scale. I glance down at the spinning numbers and then at Kim's sexy smile. "Yeah, not so good. If it goes beyond 200, I'm buying a new scale. Sure the bulge is broadening a bit, but nothing a week or two of dieting can't fix." I say as I suck in my gut.

Suddenly I hear footsteps outside the door.

"Did you say something, Don?" My wife asks.

"Uh, no."

"Could have sworn I heard you say something," she says as she walks away.

I glance down at the magazine and lower my voice.

"I know, Kim, I've got to start exercising again, gotta break out that Jane Fonda video or pump a little iron in the basement." Kim's eyes look right into mine.

I sit down on the closed toilet seat cover.

"What do you think, Kim, there's potential here. Shed about 20 pounds and I'll be a new man, a regular Kevin Costner. You know, Kevin was in here a couple months back. Drove my wife absolutely nuts. I mean, every time she went to take a shower, she threw the magazine out the door. The kids kept bringing it back, though. I'd never throw you out of my bathroom, Kim."

I get up, glance at my image in the mirror, suck in my gut once more, flex my right arm and hold my breath. I turn and look down at the magazine. Kim's expression looks as if she is desirous of my body.

I smile. "Sorry, Kim, can't have it. It's taken." I sigh and step into the bathtub.

After my shower, Kim is there waiting for me, her eyes staring at me as I dry off. It's just me and her.

"You know, Kim, I've been thinking. Maybe it isn't a good idea to be in my bathroom. I mean, if you hang around too long, my wife might get suspicious," I say as drops of water drip from my arms onto the magazine cover.

Kim just stares up at me.

"I think it is time we ended this relationship," I say softly as I hang up my towel. "I can't go on this way. I think I've reached a point in my life where I should be reading *Smithsonian* or *National Geographic* in the bathroom. I'm past my *Playboy* prime. I can't handle you young, voluptuous girls anymore. It's time I put *Time* back here."

I look down at the magazine cover. Drops of water bead up on her face. She looks as if she has been crying.

"A man must do what a man must do."

I reach down and pick up the magazine, give Kim one last close look, sigh and roll it up. I turn and throw it in the wastepaper basket next to the tub.

I put on my robe and walk out. Down the hall, my wife is sorting through the mail.

"Look a new *People*," she says holding up the magazine.

On the cover is Kathleen Turner.

I smile.

Dad's not delighted with Christmas lights

Christmas makes dads do dumb things.

They buy too many presents for their kids, thus assuring another generation of material hungry humans.

They buy too little for their wives, thus assuring another new year of marital mayhem.

And they put up Christmas decorations.

I feel safer on a ski slope than I do putting lights outside the house.

Think about it.

What if a perfect stranger came up to you and asked you to do the following...

"I want you to take this aluminum ladder and set it up on the snow and ice covering the front lawn. Forget it is 20 degrees outside with a wind chill of minus 30; forget your hands will instantly stick to the super cold metal of the ladder; forget that your body will be so cold that if you fall, your limbs will shatter like glass. Once you get to the uppermost rung, I want you to take this string of lights, with 120 volts surging through it, and with these nails and this hammer hang the lights along the eaves of the roof."

"Ya gotta be crazy!" That's what you'd say. Yet every winter thousands of men are forced to leave the comfort of their livingrooms by some primeval urge and string lights around their homes.

And not just one string.

People experience light lunacy and hang dozens of strings until their homes look like the front of some crazy carnival attraction.

I thought about this the other day when my wife told me it was time to put the Christmas lights up.

"Can't we skip it this year," I begged.

"Where's your Christmas spirit?"

"The thought of being electrocuted or falling off the ladder and ending up in a body cast somehow dampens my enthusiasm for the season. If you are so gung ho about lights, you put them up."

She glared at me.

A few minutes later, I found myself standing on the top rung of a ladder with a string of outdoor lights around my shoulders. I was leaning way forward with one leg on the ladder and the other out to the side, a counter balance of sorts.

The problem was I couldn't get close to the soffets due to the wide bushes next to the house. I had to put the ladder next to the bushes and lean over them, which sort of put a strain on the ladder's structural integrity. I started to worry about falling head first into some prickly evergreen.

One year I got creative and placed a sheet of plywood on top of the bushes and put the ladder on top of it. I managed to get onto the ladder, but upon taking one step discovered a ladder on a board on a bush is like standing on a "bongo board." My grand experiment ended with my hanging onto the eaves with a fully lighted string of bulbs wrapped around my body. I looked like some psychedelic barber's pole.

The other problem I had was putting lights above the front door. Above the door the roof rises to a peak which is just out of reach of my six-foot ladder. The only way to get lights along the roof's edge is to get onto the roof.

Scaling El Capitan in Yosemite National Park would be easier than getting on my roof and a heckuva lot safer.

Since I have no reason to go up on the roof, I have not invested in a ladder long enough to get me there. To get up onto the roof requires that I place my six-foot ladder against the chimney and scale the brick like a rock climber until I can get a handhold on the edge of the roof and pull myself up.

Nonetheless, that's what I found myself doing as I continued to string the lights. I finally got up onto the roof and began to walk toward the front of the house. Walking across a roof covered with snow was like cutting across an ice skating rink tipped on end. I knew that one false step and it would be like going down a ski jump without skis or a place to land.

To prevent that from happening I crawled across the roof on my belly. Inching toward the edge, I reached over and grabbed at the string of lights hanging a few inches below me. I moved closer to the edge, my arms fully stretched. Finally my fingers wrapped around the wire as snow holding my body gave way and gravity took me off the roof like a toboggan.

My body crashed into a large evergreen. I didn't know if the cracking I heard was ribs or branches. I paused for a moment to check if anything was broken and looked up just in time to see a glacier size sheet of snow slipping off the edge of the roof. It slammed into me like an oversized snowball, taking the entire string of lights with it.

Neighbors, who had been watching me instead of the Green Bay Packer game, came rushing out of their homes. They abruptly stopped as I lifted my body out of the evergreen. Covered with snow and brightly colored lights, I looked like a cross between the abominable snowman and Rudoph the Red Nose Reindeer. Instead of helping me, they stood laughing.

Well, at least my lights gave someone a holiday cheer.

This old house blues

When I was young and foolish, people told me that when I got married and had children I should buy a home.

A house is a great investment, they said.

A house is a great tax deduction, they said.

A house is a home you can call your own, they said.

A house is something you can own with pride, they said.

Baloney.

I've owned a house for nine years now.

The exterior walls need siding to the tune of 5 grand.

The kitchen needs remodeling—would have to sell my wife into white slavery to pay for that.

The plumbing has arteriosclerosis.

The electrical system is vintage 1950 and blows fuses like popcorn.

The kids have ruined the bedroom walls with Crayon and various sharp instruments.

And I suspect the water heater will go out any day now.

A house is sure one heck of an investment!

And my front lawn is dead, killed by a prolonged drought and years of inattention. The only green is a few weeds and some amazingly hardy crabgrass.

My house is a hypochondriac.

It is never healthy.

It isn't a structure of wood, but a living breathing monster intent on draining me of my hard earned money. I don't live in a home, I fight with a home.

Fix one thing, something else breaks.

For example, a couple of years ago I painted the outside walls. Now those same walls are peeling like some horrid skin disease.

"You've got a moisture problem, Mr. Oakland," the siding contractor says.

"Is that why the siding near the roof is warped and pulling away from the studs," I ask, not really wanting an answer.

"Yes, sir. You've got a major problem."

"How much?"

The contractor spends the next 10 minutes tapping the keys of a hand calculator. I watch his eyes widen and his head slowly shake as the numbers flash on the tiny display screen.

"Mr. Oakland, I spent the last 30 minutes walking through and around your home. You ought to seriously consider rebuilding."

"Rebuilding?"

"Your attic is so bad, Stephen King would be scared to write about it.

"Your basement is so wet, fish could thrive.

"Your bathroom has an odd odor to it.

"Your interior walls would make a ghetto graffiti artist proud.

"And, quite frankly Mr. Oakland, I don't have the guts to go poking around behind your cabinets. You know you have spiders in there who could take on Sylvester Stallone," the contractor says with a shudder.

"I'd also pave your lawn," he advises. "It is obvious you and grass don't get along.

"Yup, if I were to remodel this home, I'd use dynamite," he concludes.

My mouth drops open and I fall against the house. A section of siding cracks.

"Rotten," the contractor says.

I look up at my investment, my tax deduction, my pride and joy. "Well, at least the roof is good."

The contractor shakes his head.

"Oh, it might hold up another year or two, providing the chimney doesn't fall through it."

"Chimney?"

"Yeah, if you look closely you'll notice the mortar is dissolving and the brick is crumbling. Can't explain it. Could be old age; could be those awesome spiders."

I look down, embarrassed to ask my next question.

"Once upon a time, people told me that I should consider my first house a starter home. After a few years, I should sell it and move into a mansion, there to spend the rest of my days in peace and comfort. Maybe it's time to sell this sucker," I suggest.

The contractor laughs so hard he drops his tape measure.

"Your starter home finished a long time ago. I'd get more for my pickup than you would get for this house, unless you happen

192

to sell it to the guy on TV, you know, "This Old House." He laughs again. "He'd make a mini series out of this place."

"You know, they ought to have home health insurance," I tell the contractor. "Sort of a housing HMO. You pay a premium once a month and are covered for any major or minor repairs."

The contractor shakes his head.

"Mr. Oakland, I'm afraid your house wouldn't pass the physical."

Just then my wife comes through the backdoor.

"Donald, do you know where the sponge is? Your daughter just spilled a glass full of Coke on the livingroom carpet."

As I said, once upon a time, when I was young and foolish, I believed that owning a home was an American dream instead of a Middle Class nightmare.

Swing sets aren't simple

Before a man becomes a father, someone should take him aside, put a hand on his shoulder and offer this small piece of advice: Never ever buy your children things which aren't first assembled.

Take for instance a simple swing set.

You wouldn't think it would be much work to set one up. Wrong.

The first thing you learn is swing sets aren't as small or as light as they look. Mine came in a box nine-feet long, a package which weighed more than I did. I nearly pulled every muscle in my back trying to get the darn thing into and out of my minivan.

When unpacking a swing set, you'll quickly discover that the dozen big pieces of the structure are held together by a million assorted little pieces.

Being an organized person, I took all the assorted hardware

out of the little plastic bags they came in and neatly sorted them on a picnic table. It wasn't until I had opened the last bag that I discovered that each bag of hardware was for a particular step in the assembly process. For example, to assemble legs A and B, you were told to open hardware bag number 5396950.

Just as I was about to put all the bits and bolts away, my 3-year-old daughter jumped onto the picnic table and within seconds had every piece scattered all over the backyard.

The next day I learned that there was no way a man of my physical abilities could possibly assemble a swing set alone. Like you'd need the strength of Hercules and the digital dexterity of a concert pianist to hold together a leg and a crosspiece while trying to insert a bolt through the whole works.

I also learned you never ever assume you know what you are doing.

For a while things were going so smoothly I didn't take the time to read the instruction book. It wasn't until after I had finished and had one piece left over that I turned to the instructions and discovered that I had inadvertently fastened ladder steps to the horizontal bar supports and horizontal bars to the ladder. Heck, they all looked the same to me. Unfortunately the transposition gave the swing set an appreciable lean to the left.

Two hours and four hundred nuts and bolts later, I had the problem corrected and was ready to plant the legs into the ground.

Digging the holes was no problem. Trying to level the swing set was worse than fiddlin' with a Rubik's cube. I'd get one end level and the other end would be off; I'd get both ends level and the center would tilt.

At one point, I figured it would be easier just to stick the swing set in the ground and relandscape the entire backyard.

I was nearly exhausted when I finally got the thing reasonably level. The next step was embedding the structure into concrete. It took everything I had to drag that 60 pound bag of concrete over to the swing set and mix it. I figured one bag would surely be enough.

One bag didn't fill one-half of one hole.

I mixed up another bag.

And another.

After two trips to the hardware store, three more bags of concrete, a sore back and muscle spasms in both arms, the holes were filled and the swing set secured.

It was finally done. I crawled into a lawn chair, grabbed a beer to soothe the pain inside and rubbed massive amounts of BenGay onto my arms and legs.

My 5-year-old daughter came running into the backyard. Suddenly it all seemed worth it. "Well dear, try it out," I said with obvious pride.

"Maybe tomorrow dad. I'm going over to Melissa's house; her swing set is bigger."

Unhappiness is a house possessed

My home is possessed.

I am convinced there is an evil creature living there.

Perhaps it is the soul of my wife's cat. Long ago the cat was given away because it continually used the front hallway as an alternate litterbox. Perhaps it has come back for revenge.

It isn't a ghostly caterwauling in the night or the sound of paws crossing the kitchen floor that makes me think it is the cat. Rather it is those strange occurrences which seem to be directed at me. And as everyone in our household knows, the cat and I did not get along at all.

It started with the lawnmower.

Something robbed it of its power one day.

It would start all right, but the minute I put blade to grass, the engine would stall.

It became terribly embarrassing to cut the front lawn. I'd push the lawnmower halfway down the lawn and it would stall. I'd start it, move a couple of feet and it would stall again.

By gingerly playing with the throttle, I found I could keep the engine running, but at the slowest of speeds. After a while, I discovered that the blade was moving so slowly it was pushing the grass instead of cutting it.

My front lawn became overgrown with tall, weedy grass. It reminded me of a punk rocker's haircut. Meanwhile, the lawnmower sat in spider webs in the garage.

A few weeks later, the car started acting strangely. The transmission developed a weird whine. And it went "Ka-clunk" when I first put it in drive.

I took it into the service garage.

"Sounds fine to me," the mechanic said after he had taken the car for a drive around the block.

"Didn't you hear it?"

"Hear what?"

"The whine!"

"Nope."

The mechanic then started the engine, revved it a few times and put the car into gear. The transmission didn't make a sound.

I thanked the mechanic for his time and got into my car. As I put the transmission in drive, I heard a loud "Ka-chunk" coming from underneath the chassis.

You might think this all quite coincidental. Family cars do breakdown on occasion. And lawnmowers, particularly the cheap ones I buy, have their moments as well.

But how then do you explain a toilet which refuses to flush at night; a door that can't lock; a TV whose sound quality varies like a warped record; a dehumidifer which screams in the night, and a bathtub that can't hold its water.

I'm not kidding. All of a sudden the lock on the door to my daughters' room jammed. A few days later the drain in the bathtub jammed open. Now all we can take is showers. Then the toilet wouldn't shut off at night until you got up out of bed and jiggled the handle. And the dehumifier, which had been acting like a champ all summer, suddenly went berserk whenever its condenser motor came on.

Individually, each malfunction could be assumed to be just that, a normal malfunction. But taken in their entirety, a pattern emerged. It was as if a virus was spreading throughout my house.

The lawnmower first caught it.

While the mower was sitting in the garage, the virus spread to the car. As the car was parked in the driveway, the infection flew into the house, probably through a hole in the back door screen.

Like a demon it is corrupting and destroying as it travels through the walls. And there is no way to stop it.

I mean, if it were your traditional spirit, you could flush it out with a well placed cross or properly recited incantation. Or you could call your neighborhood exorcist. But try to find one for possessed appliances. You won't find a Yellow Pages listing for: Master Plumber/Exorcist.

At one point I stood at the top of the basement stairs and held two large pipe wrenches in the form of a cross. I must have irritated the spirit, for later that day the garbage disposal began acting up.

Unable to fight this demon, I have resigned myself to the fact that I may have to live with it for as long as our family stays in the house. My only fear is that someday the spirit might slither through the electrical wires and find its way into my computer and xhjopiuo oudopfiuoiuc -jlii1132iioji iul sss hi mom g.a.iui.....xxxx.../ ///5/aus...

197

The wild breakfast olympics

Watching countless hours of Winter Olympic action on the tube began to affect me in strange and mysterious ways.

Some of the effects lingered long after the games had finished.

Like the other day when I was making breakfast, I suddenly found my mind wandering. The next thing I knew I was standing in front of a hot griddle at the center of a large arena in Calgary.

Next to me were Dick Button and Jim McKay. Dick began speaking into a microphone.

"Well, Jim, you can just feel the excitement and tension in the audience tonight as Don Oakland tries for a gold medal in the pancake flipping competition. He is the USA's only hope for a medal in this event."

"Dick, if anyone can do it, Oakland can," McKay said enthusiastically. "He's been training long and hard. In fact, let's take a moment to take a look at this young man 'Close up and Personal.'"

Onto the TV screen came a picture of me cooking pancakes on a campfire in Canada. McKay started his narration.

"Don Oakland got his start cooking pancakes while fishing with his buddies in Canada. Although he liked flipping flapjacks, he lacked a certain degree of timing..."

The TV showed a griddle of pitch black pancakes.

"In fact, his brother-in-law once used Don's pancakes for a different kind of sport," McKay said as the screen showed my brother-in-law whipping one of my pancakes like a Frisbie across the lake.

"However, once Don began using an electric griddle, his pancake flipping skills increased dramatically, and after years of practice, he is now a world-class competitor," McKay concluded as the TV coverage returned to the arena.

"Don Oakland is second behind Bo Swenson of Sweden. Don was leading after the eight-inch heavyweight pancake flipping event, but he had a little trouble in the three-inch mini event. He flipped one of those little flapjacks just a little too hard and it landed like a monocle in the left eye of one of the judges," Button reported.

The camera focused on me as I flipped a five-inch pancake high above the griddle.

"A nice flip, but it was just a hair early, Jim. Notice the slight splatter as the pancake hit the griddle. He'll surely lose points. In fact, if he is to catch Bo Swenson of Sweden, he'll have to do something pretty dramatic," Button said with a sigh.

"You remember last year, Oakland tried a triple flip and it went so high it stuck on the ceiling. It was so embarrassing, he dropped out of competition. It wasn't until after several sessions with a pancake psychotherapist that he was able to get his confidence back. What a come back story it has been," Dick said melodramatically.

"Wait! What's this! Don Oakland is attempting a triple flip, behind the back double flip—something never seen before in Olympic competition. There it goes...one, two, three... and he catches it on the spatula behind his back. He flips it up again... one and two and back on the griddle it goes... Jim! He did it! He made Olympic history and captured the gold...What an exciting day this is!"

Suddenly my mind flipped back to the present. I looked down and saw four perfectly round, perfectly black pancakes. Reality hurts sometimes, it really does.

The Winter Olympics Northwoods style

You know what we need? Some real Winter Olympics.

I'm talking about new sports that would put some meat behind the "thrill of victory and the agony of defeat." Games that would make ski jumpers and bobsledders look like pansies.

I'm talking about competition based on the reality of north country winters.

I'm talking about sidewalk skating.

I'm talking about heavyweight car pushing.

I'm talking about marathon snow shoveling.

I'm talking about speed scraping.

Allow me to elaborate.

Sidewalk skating would be a game of balance, finesse and breath-taking acrobatics.

The competitors would assume this "real life" situation: It's 6:30 in the morning, you're running late and as you grab your coat you hear the city bus coming. You fly out of the house, clear the steps in a single bound only to find yourself on a sidewalk of glare ice.

Competitors would be judged on how well they recover from the jump off the stairs and how quickly they can "skate" their way down the sidewalk. They must reach the finish line— which simulates an icy curb— within two minutes or they "miss the bus" and are disqualified.

It would be a thrilling sport to watch as competitors flail their arms and twist their bodies to recover their balance and maintain forward momentum. It would be a dangerous sport because as anyone who grew up in the northwoods knows, ice ain't soft.

Car pushing would resemble weightlifting with a couple of odd variations. Competitors would be placed in different weight classes. Lightweights would be required to "push" a Yugo out of a snowbank and up a street with a slight incline, a street covered with six inches of snow and ice. Heavyweights would be required to push a Cadillac up the same street.

Not only would competitors have to be strong, but they would need to be surefooted on ice and be knowledgeable about how to put one's shoulder to the rear fender of a car.

Again this would be a thrilling sport to watch as competitors' slip and are runover by backsliding cars.

In marathon snow shoveling, competitors would take racing shovels and clear sidewalks around a city block. The sidewalks would be covered with 12 inches of heavy, wet snow.

I can just hear Jim McKay doing the commentary...

"And here comes Lars McSmith from Bemidji, Minnesota, rounding the last corner, he is at least two driveways ahead of his nearest opponent. Lars has been shoveling for 52.6.88 minutes. At this pace he'll surely set a new world's record...

"Oh my, Lars just went down. He's lying face down in a snowbank, his specially designed lightweight Kevlar shovel is sticking straight up from between his legs. I don't know exactly what happened, perhaps this instant replay will show us...

"Here comes Lars, he's looking awfully good, his arms moving that shovel like a piston...Oh my gosh!" On the screen, we see Lars' shovel blade catching a crack in the sidewalk causing the shovel to abruptly stop. The momentum sends Lars' body right into the shovel, its handle slamming into his stomach like a knight's lance. Jim continues his commentary: "Let's watch in slow motion as Lars recoils from the pain and crumbles like dry paper into the snow bank....

"And here comes the pack behind him, shoveling with every bit of energy they possess. Look at the clouds of snow their shovels are throwing into the air...And lying motionless in the snowbank is...is...hey where's Lars! My gosh! They have covered him with at least two feet of snow...rescue workers are rushing to the scene...all we can see of Lars is the very tip of his shovel handle...what a heartbreak for the Bemidji Broadshoveler."

The last event would require explosive speed, agility and strength. Like a summer sprint, it would be an event measured in seconds.

Competitors would be lined up in front of a row of Buicks which had been left out all night. When the gun sounded, the competitors would run to the front of the cars, brandish their ice scrapers and proceed to clean the front windshields. I could see them using razor sharp, high-tech scrapers to remove the ice in seconds.

It would be poetry in motion to watch these men and women scrape one half of the window, then fling their bodies over the front hood to scrape the other half.

If nothing else, the window scrapping event might encourage U.S. businesses to develop better window scrapers than we have now. I envision scrapers autographed and endorsed by Gold Medal Olympic scrapers.

Yup, I think it is time for more realistic olympics. I mean, if we can have Lumberjack Olympics we ought to have olympics for those of us who survive winters year after year.

And training facilities would be dirt cheap.

Heck, I'd be willing to lend out my driveway and sidewalk for an aspiring marathon snow shoveler in need of training.

How to make writing risky

Being a writer/editor is not an exciting profession. It is a rewarding one, but the work is not very exotic or risky or macho in any way.

I mean, the most excitement I experience around the office is when an occasional typo surfaces, like the unfortunate insertion of one too many letters in the name of the company's president or writing January 14, 1899 when January 4, 1989 is the correct date.

It is indeed fortunate that nothing a writer/editor does causes physical injury or death. Otherwise, there would be bodies strewn throughout our department.

I'm consoled by the fact that in the scheme of things, nothing I write will have a major impact. Civil wars won't break out; plagues won't descend upon the land and financial ruin won't occur. About all I ever cause is a minor nuisance.

When I worked for a newspaper, there was at least the risk of libeling someone.

"Don, will you please step into my office for a minute," the editor says with a grim expression across his face.

I walk into his office, unaware of two powerfully dressed attorneys right behind me.

"Now about this article you wrote about Mr. Smith," the editor says, pulling a clipping of the article from a manila folder. "You wrote that in 1984, Mr. Smith was convicted of drunken driving."

"He was," I reply.

"He wasn't," the editor growls.

"He wasn't?"

"He wasn't."

"Oh."

The editor reaches into another folder and pulls out a long document.

"Mr. Smith is suing us for $2 million."

"Two million!" I gasp. My body suddenly loses its strength and slumps into the chair.

"Mr. Smith says because of the article he lost his job, his wife left him and his creditors are descending upon him like vultures.

"I thought sure I read that court document correctly," I say shaking my head.

One of the attorneys behind me opens up his briefcase and pulls out two documents.

"It appears, Mr. Oakland took the information for said

article from the minutes of this court appearance by Donald J. Smith, who was convicted of drunken driving. However, the article Mr. Oakland wrote dealt with a Donald C. Smith, who has never been to court in his life."

"An honest mistake," I suggest.

The attorneys laugh quietly.

"OK, plead temporary insanity," I say as I squirm in my chair.

"Two million dollars, that's half the assets of the newspaper," the editor moans as he drops his head into his hands.

"Gee, I'm awfully sorry," I say softly.

The editor just glares at me.

The lawyers just smile. They know the fees they'll make defending the newspaper will pay their salaries for the next two years.

Anyway, as I was saying, being a writer/editor is not as exciting as being a general assignment reporter.

Therefore, I have had to inject some excitement into my job.

I do it in small ways.

Every so often, I will go back into the storeroom and turn off the lights. Then I'll take the pot of coffee brewing on the coffemaker and attempt to pour it into the cup I'm holding. Pouring black coffee in a dark room is a real challenge, a challenge with certain attendant risks.

One time I screamed so loud after pouring hot coffee on my hand, I brought the entire administrative staff of the department running to the storeroom. Luckily I was able to flick on the light before anyone arrived.

Eventually I became quite good at pouring coffee in the dark.

I had to first master blindly aligning the pot with the cup.

That's akin to bringing the fingers of two hands together while your eyes are shut.

I accomplished this feat by placing myself in an almost meditative trance. I pictured in my mind the pot and cup floating through the universe.

A secretary once popped into the storeroom just as I was about to pour and flicked on the light. After she regained her composure, she concluded that I must have been on drugs.

The second challenge I had to master was not to overfill the cup. This required refinement of hearing and feeling. I found after much trial and error and scalded knuckles, that the sound of a half-filled cup is different from the sound of a nearly full cup. I tried to explain this to a co-worker once, but she just gave me a strange look and walked away.

The third challenge I had to meet was getting the nearly full cup back to my desk without spilling it.

I used deep breathing and Zen chants to accomplish this feat. As I walked down the corridor of our department, I took slow, deep breaths and murmured "Aaaa nay nay nay zoooooooo nay nay zooooo nay nay."

I am proud to report this technique has been very successful. The only time I spill coffee is when I chance to encounter someone in the hallway.

"Don! Speak up if you have something to say," an executive vice president once said to me as I walked by him with my coffee cup in hand.

"Uh, no I wasn't speaking to you sir, I was, was, uh, conjugating the verb to be, yeah, conjugating," I replied as I tried to wipe spilled coffee off my tie and pants.

As I said, when you are a writer you have to add a little risk-taking to your job.

The sweet seduction of a dieter

The first of the year, I went on a diet and suddenly became surrounded by sweets.

I'm not kidding. It was the strangest thing.

The first rule of dieting is to give up all those things you really like: cookies, cakes, puddings and pastry. And that's what I did.

It wasn't hard. All I had to do was condition myself not to have dessert after every meal, something I had been doing since I was 2.

My body seemed to tolerate my sweet-tooth. I could eat any dessert, indulge in any snack and not gain an ounce of weight. Through high school, I remained basically a beanpole. In college, I filled out a little, but there was some muscle mixed in, the remnants of an ill-fated season on the gymnastics team. Even when I entered the world of work, weight was not a problem.

However, as I approach 40, this marvelous metabolism of mine seems to be slowing down as the scales seem to be speeding up.

A size 16 shirt suddenly became too small; a once loose fitting pair of pants, suddenly became tight. My body was announcing the end of an era, the end of carefree, or careless, eating.

Being a conservative person (aka: cheapskate), I opted not to buy a diet book or join a weight reduction program. I just resolved to remove sweets and down-size servings.

Then something happened. Sweets came out of the woodwork.

I'd open the refrigerator and there next to the milk would be a plastic bag filled with Christmas cookies. And next to the bread box would be a plastic container of more Christmas cookies.

I'd go to the cupboard for a can of soup and be confronted by a box of Girl Scout cookies, the richest, most caloric, best tasting Girl Scout cookies you could buy.

I'd rush into the livingroom to escape temptation only to find my 3-year-old nibbling on an Oreo. Next to her on the end table were three more Oreos.

I reached for my coat. I needed to get out of the house; I needed to take a drive. I reached in my pocket for the car keys and pulled out a Snickers bar instead.

My daughter gave me an odd look as I bolted out the door, ran through the snow and jumped into the car. Safe at last, I said to myself. Then I glanced down and saw a can of pop sitting on the dash. It wasn't diet. Next to it was a package of gum. It wasn't sugarless. And on the floor was a six-pack of Milky Ways.

I was torn.

Do I throw everything out or eat it?

Do I destroy those cookies which my wife and my mother-in-law spent hours painstakingly making?

Do I throw out those Girl Scout cookies which I spent a small fortune on?

Do I deny my children candy because of weak-willed appetite?

As I contemplated these questions, I sat at the kitchen table finishing off a box of gourmet chocolates which someone at work had given me. Until that moment, I never knew how much guilt chocolate could cause.

Work was no different.

One morning while I sat at my desk, a secretary dropped by and gave me a danish covered with sweet white icing and filled with rich custard. It was leftover from a meeting of executives. (Business executives are an odd bunch. They schedule "breakfast meetings," have their secretaries order large platters of pastry and then never touch it. It's as if this is some way of showing they have the "right stuff." Trouble is I end up with the sweet stuff on my desk.)

Lunch was hard because the first thing you encountered in the Cafeteria line were the desserts. When you were most hungry, you had to pass by cakes, cookies, pies and puddings.

Everywhere there were sweets.

In my dreams, there were sweets.

On TV there were sweets.

In magazines there were sweets.

In the stores there were sweets. What is the last thing you pass by in a grocery store? *The National Enquirer* and a rack full of candy.

Sweets on the streets— teenagers standing on the corners consuming candy bars by the gross.

I have found only one antidote to sweets: Beer.

I can't stand eating anything sweet while drinking beer. I mean, the thought of beer with a Baby Ruth or a chocolate covered donut is repulsive.

Beer is the only thing which has helped me fight the seduction of sweets. But now I've got another problem.

THE CREATURE COMFORTS CHRONICLES

I'm a victim of videos

Home videos are giving me headaches.

Today it seems everywhere you go someone is trying to rent or sell you a video of *Batman*.

Time was I went to the grocery store for food and other household supplies. Now when I go it's for meat, milk, veggies and videos. It has added a new, unnerving dimension to shopping, especially when the kids are along.

The instant we pass through the front door of the grocery store, my 5-year-old heads full tilt for the video department. Before I can catch up with her, she already has a half dozen video cassettes in her arms.

"No videos today," I tell her sternly. "I bought you one the last time we were in the store."

"But daddy, I haven't seen *Strawberry Shortcake's Greatest Adventure*," she pleads as she drops all but one video to the floor.

"No!" I respond as I recall simpler times when all she wanted during a trip to the store was a stick of gum at the checkout.

"Pleeeease!"

"Not today, maybe the next time we're in the store," I tell her as I take the video from her.

My attempt at compromise only results in my daughter throwing one of her better tantrums, much to the amusement of everyone else in the store.

Suddenly, she grabs the video out of my hand and bolts for the exit. Next thing I know buzzers are going off and several clerks are in hot pursuit of my daughter.

She makes it through the produce section, successfully dodges a clerk in the meat department, but is stopped by a roadblock clerks had set up in canned goods.

I rush back to the video counter, quickly plunk down enough cash to rent the movie and dash off to bail out my fugitive daughter.

When I get home, I discover the video she picked out is only 30 minutes long. I'd paid the same amount for a video two hours long. I tell you it ain't fair.

My problems with videos don't end there.

Every Sunday night my wife and I treat ourselves to a video. It's our reward for making it through the week. However, sometimes our evening becomes less than relaxing.

"Donald, how could you!" My wife screams as she lifts the video out of the grocery bag.

"What's wrong with *Robocop*?"

"It's disgusting."

"It's science fiction, a satirical look at a scenario of the future."

"Baloney! It's mindless violence; it's gross, and I refuse to watch it!"

"But, dear it is one of the most popular videos."

211

"So there are a lot of warped people out there, that doesn't mean you have to bring trash like this home. Why didn't you pick out something like *Dirty Dancing* or *Stake-out*?"

At that point I retreat into the kitchen and then return with another video.

"Just in case you didn't want *Robocop*, I got another movie..."

"What?" my wife asks suspiciously.

"*Predator*?"

Well, she gives me a look that would have put the fear of God into Arnold Schwarzenegger. She looks as if she is going to kill me on the spot. Instead she just shakes her head, goes into the bedroom, jumps into bed and begins reading a book. "Heck, it's one of Arnold's better films," I plead with her through the locked door.

Thanks to home videos, I feel like our marriage is becoming a sequel to Siskel and Ebert.

Video virus hits Uncle Harry

"Absolutely not!"

"But dear, having one would be a lot of fun and it would be an ideal way to record the growth of our children.

"No."

"Is it the cost?" I ask.

"No."

"Then what?"

"I don't want you becoming another Uncle Harry," my wife says.

Uncle Harry is a new breed of amateur photojournalist. Every technological improvement in photography produces a new generation of Uncle Harrys.

When the snapshot camera came out, Uncle Harry was the

first to get one. He shot pictures of every member of his family and every animate and inanimate object within focusing distance. And every shot he'd carefully tape to the pages of an album which he would share with you for hours and hours and hours on end. When the home movie camera came out, Uncle Harry was there with his Super 8 filming every family activity. He was worse than Geraldo Rivera. No one could escape his zoom lens. And later he would show you his movies for hours and hours and hours on end.

Then came 35mm slide film and Uncle Harry with his Japanese SLR. Roll upon roll he'd shoot. He was an annoyance at first, but after he bought a motor drive he was obnoxious. A child's birthday party was worth two rolls of 36-exposures; a picnic was good for a 24-exposure roll, and a trip out west produced no less than 10 rolls of slides which he would put in his self-focusing Carousel projector and show you for hours and hours and hours on end.

Now Uncle Harry has a camcorder.

You always know when Uncle Harry arrives at the party. The room suddenly becomes bathed in the bright light from the photoflood lamp atop his VHS camcorder.

Uncle Harry was a nuisance with his Brownie, a pain with his Super 8 and obnoxious with his SLR. But with a camcorder in his hands, Harry is down right dangerous.

You see, Harry doesn't know when to stop filming. He doesn't know when to turn off the microphone. He just moves through the room shooting whatever he manages to get in focus.

Armed with a powerful zoom lens and a sensitive microphone, he has the ruthlessness of a CIA operative. He eavesdrops on conversations and catches embarrassing gestures or social gaffes.

That wouldn't be so bad, but he insists on showing everything he shoots to anyone who will sit in front of his television for hours and hours and hours on end.

Editing is a dirty word to Uncle Harry.

His videos give you headaches because your eyes are subjected to the blurred images he produces when he forgets to turn off the camera as he turns around, or as he temporarily loses his balance or as someone brushes up against him.

My favorite Uncle Harry video was a 50th wedding anniversary party he decided to document.

Halfway through the party, Uncle Harry decided to give his camera a rest and raid the buffet table. Unfortunately, he forgot to turn the camera off.

My wife and I watched in horror as the camera captured pictures of people's rear ends and legs as Harry carried the camera like a suitcase at his side. We gasped as the camera swung toward the buffet table and gave us a nearly microscopic view of a platter of pasta salad.

We listened as the microphone surreptitiously picked up a conversation between two cousins of the honored couple who were remarking how after 50 years of marriage the husband looked overweight and harried and the wife looked like a cast member of "The Night of the Living Dead."

Uncle Harry loved it. As long as the pictures were in focus, he loved it.

It didn't bother him that his camera caught Aunt Sarah's 5-year-old taking a pee behind the shelter house.

It didn't bother him that he put onto a 25-inch TV screen with full stereo sound a picture of Cousin Ted belching .

It didn't bother him that he captured in full color brother Paul catching a football pass halfway between the bellybutton and the kneecap and all the facial contortions which followed.

It didn't bother him that he caught the honored husband casting a rather lurid glance at a well-endowed teenage girl who went rollerskating by wearing tight red shorts and a t-shirt cut at the midriff.

Uncle Harry had 4-hours of tape to fill and by golly he wasn't going to put his camcorder away until every minute was filled.

There are a lot of Uncle Harrys out there.

And more are on the way.

They'll be there filming the Christmas pageants.

Their lights will bleach out graduations and weddings.

Their super sensitive mics will be recording your conversations and playing them back to you as embarrassment sends you sinking into the sofa.

They will take the romance out of remembrances.

With a photograph there is a single image and a story to tell. With a video, all the images are there— the entire story unfolds on the screen without embellishment or discretion.

But Uncle Harrys don't care. The joy is in the filming, the capturing of every nuance of a scene. Uncle Harrys take pride in their technical expertise and not the visual chaos they bring to the TV screen.

And it is because of the Uncle Harrys out there, that my wife won't let me buy a camcorder. She tells me I do enough damage with my SLR.

How to computerize Christmas

"Your computer is ruining our Christmas," my wife complained as she slammed the door to my office and stomped up to the kitchen.

All I did was make a tiny suggestion on how we might save time sending out Christmas cards.

I raced up the stairs after her.

"Look dear, what is the purpose of Christmas cards?" I asked her.

"Cards are a way of sharing news about the family and to pass along a bit of Christmas spirit," she said as she started doing the dishes.

"That's what I'm suggesting we do..."

"Donald, Christmas cards are a very personal thing. What you're suggesting has about as much personal touch as a letter from the IRS."

"On the contrary, my cards would be personal..."

"Personalized," she interrupted. "A letter from mom is personal; a letter from Ed McMahon is personalized. Look, I'm willing to compromise. I did agree to let you put our Christmas card mailing list on computer and use mailing labels. But that's it."

I sat down at the kitchen table, unwrapped a small Christmas candy cane intended for my 3-year-old's Christmas stocking, and pondered my arguments as I sucked on the candy.

I took a deep breath and began my proposal again.

"Every year, we sit down and put together a Christmas card letter which highlights all the things we did over the past year. And after we type it up, we take it down to the printer's and have 50 copies made which we then enclose in every card we mail out..."

"Remember, dear, I also add a personal note to many of the cards," my wife interrupted.

"Right. So why not put together all those little personal notes into my database, index them, and combine them into a format of a Christmas letter..."

"I tell you, the Grinch has nothing on Donald Oakland," my wife muttered.

"By using the database on my computer, we can personalize each Christmas letter. For example, using the mail merge feature, I can insert your Aunt's and Uncle's name at the beginning and anywhere in the body of their Christmas letter. Then I could program into the computer instructions to insert your 'personal comments' drawn from the database. Just tell it to insert comments A1, C2, D5 and H4 and wha-la you have a customized Christmas letter."

"Donald, I really don't want to hear this again."

"Look, we could mail out twice as many customized Christmas letters than traditional Christmas letters."

"Yeah, and they would have all the warmth of a Styrofoam cup!"

"Comeon, this way we can give our friends and relatives the maximum amount of information about our family in the least amount of time."

"Donald, they don't want to read a book about us!"

"No problem. We could input into the computer short and long letters. We could have letters that have a lot about the kids or letters with more information about us. We just tell the computer which letter to print for which person."

"I'd like to input your ideas...input them right into the nearest snowbank. Half the fun of Christmas is sending and receiving Christmas cards," she said, her voice showing increasing impatience.

"Why can't you forget that stupid computer of yours and think about us as a family. Why not come out of the basement once in awhile and do something with your family. Why can't we all sit around the livingroom table, with cups of hot chocolate and Christmas cookies next to us, and write out Christmas cards. It would be such a warm, family activity to do during the Christmas season. The girls could even take part by signing their names."

"Now there's an idea!" I shouted.

My wife smiled like a lawyer who just convinced a jury of her client's innocence.

"I could digitize our signatures, the girls' included, and merge them into the letters. Wow!"

My wife suddenly turned from the sink, grabbed me by my shirt collar and lifted me out of the chair. She threw open the back door and with her right foot sent me flying into a large snowbank.

"Donald Oakland, you're hopeless!" She yelled as she slammed the door.

Toys are becoming technologically troublesome

I'm sorry, but I can't get excited over electronic toys.

I admit some are educational wonders.

I'll concede they are pretty sophisticated, some rivaling minicomputers of years back.

But one thing they aren't is durable.

Electronics and kids just don't get along.

A couple years back we bought one of our daughters a talking doll. It was an amazing toy. Its lips synched perfectly with the recorded speech. Its eyes moved. It looked like something you might find at Disneyland.

Then one day, Little Miss Electronic Marvel took a tumble down the stairs.

Little Miss Electronic Marvel suddenly developed a speech impediment. The words came forth, but the lips never moved. "Great! A ventriloquist doll," I muttered to myself.

Then one day, Little Miss Electronic Marvel suffered cardiac arrest. Her batteries died. Seems one of the kids left the tape player running all night.

I soon discovered health care for a talking doll is expensive. Cabbage Patch dolls come with papers. Talking dolls should come with health insurance policies.

I could buy a case of premium beer for what it would cost me to replace Little Miss Electronic Marvel's batteries.

So there Little Miss Electronic Marvel sat. Once she stopped talking, the kids lost interest in her. Once I found out how much it would cost to repair and repower her, I lost interest.

Some day, perhaps when my daughters are a little older, I will bring Little Miss Electronic Marvel back to life.

Kid computers are no less bothersome.

A while back I bought my eldest girl an "educational computer."

It was really slick.

Stick a card in, press a button or two and it taught shapes and words and colors and a whole lot more.

And most importantly, my daughter loved it. She would play with it for 15 minutes, an amazing accomplishment considering my daughter's attention span. I mean, my daughter is the only kid I know whose attention span is measured in nanoseconds.

Then one day the 3-year-old got at it.

I don't know what she did, but the computer is now saying yes to everything, even wrong answers. Sometimes it never quits. It just runs and runs and runs.

How do you fix something like that?

In the good old days, you could go down to the hardware store, pick up a couple of nuts and bolts and fix a toy. There wasn't anything a screw driver, hammer and airplane glue couldn't fix.

I don't know about you, but there is nothing around the Oakland household I could use to fix a memory chip.

Once I took a computer game to an electrical repair shop. I've never seen anyone laugh so hard as that repairman did. "Send it back to the company," he said between bursts of laughter.

So I did.

And the company wrote back that it would cost $30 plus shipping to repair it.

I only paid $28 for the thing new.

After slamming my head against the wall and screaming at the ceiling, I sent in the $30 bucks.

Eight weeks later, the computer toy arrived.

I couldn't tell if it was fixed or not. The battery I had sent with it was gone.

After slamming my head against the wall and screaming at the ceiling, I went to the hardware store for another battery. I put the $1.50 battery inside the computer and it worked.

I gave it to my daughter who immediately began playing with it.

Next morning, my daughter handed me the computer toy. "It doesn't work," she said sadly.

I glanced at the switch underneath. It was in the ON position.

I asked my daughter to leave the room. Then after slamming my head against the wall and screaming at the ceiling, I popped the dead battery out and headed off to the hardware store.

When I returned, I found the 3-year-old playing with the computer in the middle of the kitchen floor. I scooped it up, ran into my bedroom and locked the door. I put in the battery and pressed a button. The computer should have responded affirmatively. Instead it flashed "INCORRECT" across its LED screen and kept flashing the message until I pulled the battery from its socket.

After slamming my head against the wall and screaming at the ceiling, I placed the computer toy— minus the battery— on a shelf in the playroom.

To this day, it still sits on that shelf. It is a testament to the fragility of high tech.

I'm a veteran of video violence

A new form of consumer conflict is emerging.

I call it video violence.

If you think shopping on a Sunday just before Christmas is risky, you ought to try buying a popular video on a Friday night.

It gets down right ugly. I know; I've been there...

I knew my 5-year-old and I would be in for a firefight when we entered the DVZ— the Demilitarized Video Zone. The aisles were crowded. Twice as many videos were going out as were coming in. The shelves were starting to thin out.

As I stood there assessing the situation from a tactical point of view, my daughter— always on the offensive when she enters the battle zone— disappeared down one of the aisles.

A few moments later I heard her crying.

"Good grief, wounded already!" I said to myself as I pushed aside a small boy and dashed down the aisle.

My daughter was standing next to another little girl about her size. "Daddy! She took my *An American Tail* !" my daughter screamed.

The little girl clutched her video close to her chest and gave my daughter a nasty look.

My daughter gave a few glances right and left, then attacked. She swooped down on the little girl and grabbed the video from her hands with all the skill of a football player prying the ball away from an opponent. The little girl instantly started crying.

"Hey! You can't do that," I said taking the video from my daughter. "It's not nice and it's not fair."

As I was handing the video back to the little girl, I felt a hand grab the back of my shirt collar. Before I knew it, my feet were off the ground, and I was face to face with a rather large and very angry looking man. I quickly surmised that this man, who looked like he belonged in center ring of All-Star Wrestling, was the father of the little girl.

"Hey creep! Where do you get off taking my little girl's tape?" He growled.

"I was merely returning it, sir," I replied in a quiet, innocent voice. " You see, my daughter exercising a certain degree of misjudgment, took it from your daughter."

"What daughter?"

I looked around. My daughter was nowhere to be found. I looked up at the man, his face turning redder and redder. I was just about to reach for my wallet to pay for the little girl's tape when...

"Harold!"

The big man put me down and turned toward a rather

frantic looking woman. "Harold, that man just took my *Beetlejuice*," she said pointing to a thin, balding fellow moving toward the checkout.

"Don't go away," he growled and then took after that little man like a killer shark. I glanced around the room and spotted my daughter. I ran over to her, scooped her up into my arms and retreated out of the store.

***

At certain times, video stores resemble aquariums filled with fish in a feeding frenzy. Like the instant the clerk puts *ET* on the shelf, two dozen people converge on it.

To win at that game, you have to be smart.

If I'm after a popular video, I'll hang out near the checkout counter rather than the "New Releases" section. Veterans of video warfare quickly learn battles are won or lost before videos even get checked in.

Let me tell you about one such video victory for which I should have received a Video Valor medal.

My mission was to return home with a *Beetlejuice* video, which at the time was the second most popular video. It was so popular, unless you went looking for it on a Wednesday night during a blizzard, you'd never see it on the shelves.

I set up my position just west of the return counter. Not wanting to appear conspicuous, I made like I was carefully browsing the National Geographic tapes.

Instinctively, I glanced up just in time to spot a lady returning six tapes, one of them being *Bettlejuice*. I initiated my assault immediately. My eyes never left the video as the clerk took it from the lady, set it on the counter and checked it in with a bar code reader.

Suddenly out of the corner of my eye, I saw another woman moving in. She, too, was interested in *Beetlejuice*.

I knew I had to act quickly because the lady was closer to the counter than I was. I knew this competition would be decided before the video reached the return cart.

"Hey! Whose kid is falling out of that shopping cart over there!" I yelled.

The woman stopped for a second, turned to see if it was her kid and then turned back to the counter. Unfortunately for her that was all the time I needed to snatch *Beetlejuice* from the clerk's hand.

"Can I please have that *Beetlejuice* tape that just came in," the lady said unaware of my brilliant maneuver.

"I'm sorry ma'am, this gentleman just checked it out," the clerk said and turned to another customer.

The woman gave me a dirty look and walked away.

I took out a pocket knife and notched another "kill" on my video membership card.

Terror between the trees

I think it's high time Hollywood recognizes the Wisconsin as an ideal place to film a horror movie.

May I suggest... "The Hunter's Horror"— or— "Terror Between the Trees..."

It was the opening day of deer season. Sam, his two teenage buddies, Charlie and Harry, and their girlfriends, Kate, Lucy and Mary, sat by the fireplace at Sam's hunting shack near Tomahawk, Wisconsin. The guys swapped deer stories as they passed around a bottle of brandy. The girls giggled and wondered out loud how their boyfriends convinced them to come along on their very first deer hunt. Nevertheless, they were having fun because being in the shack reminded them of the slumber parties they had as kids.

"Yup, tomorrow I'm going to get that 10-pointer," Sam boasted. "I'm going to take my 30-30 and bring him down with one shot through the shoulders."

"Ha!" Charlie said as he bit into a piece of beef jerky. "You

223

couldn't hit the broadside of a buffalo."

"You watch, my man, you just watch."

"Uh, Sam, where's the bathroom," Kate asked.

Sam laughed. "Remember that small little building that you said was so cute."

"You got to be kidding," the girl gasped as she turned to Mary hoping she would say that Sam was just kidding. Being a city girl herself, Mary seemed just as horrified.

Sam handed the girl a flashlight. She put on a blaze orange coat and walked outside into the knee deep snow. She pulled the collar up around her ears as the wind ripped through the jack pines and aspen.

Suddenly she stopped.

"Sam?" she said quietly.

No reply came, just the gentle rush of the wind.

"Is that you, Sam," she said, nervously shining the light into the darkness.

Still no reply.

She began to slowly back up toward the door of the shack. Suddenly the brush behind her exploded and out jumped a shadowy creature. She screamed.

Sam and his friends rushed out of the shack, their flashlights wildly cutting across the dark woods. "Kate! Kate! Where are you?" Sam cried out.

No reply.

"Sam, look here!" Harry yelled.

Sam and his friends bent over the snow and pointed their flashlights at a torn piece of blaze orange fabric surrounded by tiny pools of blood about the size of quarters.

"Get inside!" Sam yelled. "Harry, get your gun. Charlie, you take my Jeep into town and get help."

Charlie grabbed his rifle and a full clip of ammunition. He jumped into the car and stomped on the accelerator. The Jeep spun around and shot off into the darkness.

Charlie could barely see the two rut road as he drove

through the woods. It was sure eerie driving on a road without streetlights, signs or other cars, he thought to himself.

Suddenly the headlights caught two buttons of light which leaped out from behind a stand of pines. Charlie jerked the wheel left to avoid what he knew was a deer attracted by the lights. The vehicle jumped out of the ruts and slid up against a small maple.

Charlie shook his head; then looked in the rearview mirror to see if he had been cut. He was all right.

"Well, it's about 50 yards to the main road," he said to himself as he got out of the Jeep. "Might as well walk to the road rather than go back to the cabin."

He grabbed his flashlight and rifle and started down the two rut road.

It was quiet in the woods. The wind had died down. Away from the brilliance of the Jeep's headlights, Charlie could see stars above and the moon rising over the treetops.

He stopped.

There was a rustling sound just to his left.

"A deer," he said to himself. " A big one at that."

He snapped the lever of his rifle forward and back, sending a cartridge into the chamber. He held the rifle in his right hand and slowly moved the flashlight in his other hand.

Suddenly the beam of light fell on two fiery red eyes and a huge rack of horns. The horns shot forward as Charlie swung his gun.

Blam!

The horns of the creature caught the barrel of the rifle just as it discharged. The bullet shot skyward; it clipped off several branches and sent a huge chunk of snow crashing down on Charlie.

Charlie brushed the snow from his face and looked up.

"AAAAAIIEEEEEEE!"

He scrambled out of the snow pile and took off running down the road. He could hear the creature right behind him, but he was too scared to look back. He jumped off the road and dove for a nearby tree limb. Like an Olympic gymnast, he swung his body up and over the branch.

"Go away you devil deer!" Charlie shouted at the pair of glowing red eyes looking up at him. "Let me live and I promise I'll never shoot another deer in my life. I'll even put my Dodge Dart in the ditch should I ever encounter one of your brothers on the highway. I swear..."

Meanwhile back at the cabin.

"Did you hear that shot?" Mary asked, looking anxiously out the window.

"Nah. It was probably a tree branch breaking from the weight of snow," Harry said.

"I'm scared..."

The girl abruptly stopped. "What's that sound?"

"What sound?" Sam asked.

"That scraping sound."

The four teenagers stood very still.

A strange sound was coming from behind the front door. Sam cocked his rifle.

"Who's there?" he yelled.

No reply.

"Say something or I'll shoot!"

The girls huddled close to Harry, their eyes fixed on the door, their ears hearing nothing but the ominous scratching sound coming from the other side.

Blam!

Sam's shot blew through the top of the door. It was high enough that it would have gone over the head of a man, but close enough to scare anyone away, anyone sane that is.

The scraping sound continued.

Blam!

Sam aimed a foot lower.

The scraping sound continued.

Blam Blam!!

This time the shots were aimed much lower, low enough to

hit a man below the shoulders. The scraping stopped.

"I think you got him," Harry said weakly.

"Don't know."

"Better go check."

"No!" Mary screamed. "Please Sam, don't open that door."

"Don't worry, Mary... Harry will back me up." Harry pushed the girls aside and leveled his rifle at the doorway. Sam put his gun down and slowly turned the knob. He whipped opened the door and... nothing, just the blackness of the night. He shone the flashlight on the blanket of snow.

"Only thing out here are our boot tracks and...say...will you look at the size of these deer tracks!"

Suddenly a black form shot out from the brush, slammed into Sam's body and carried him into the shack.

"AAAAAAAAIE!" Sam screamed as the horns of a huge buck dug into his chest. The massive buck flicked its head, sending Sam's body crashing through the kitchen table.

Harry took aim, but before his finger could pull the trigger, the big buck was on him, its deadly 12-point rack pinning him against the floor.

"Help me!" Harry screamed.

Lucy frantically ran to the kitchen, jumped over Sam's unconscious body and grabbed a butcher knife from a cupboard. She raised the knife above her head and charged the big deer.

The deer turned its head quickly, the tips of its horns slashing across the girl's blouse, ripping it to shreds (I'm sorry folks, but this type of movie requires at least one open blouse scene no matter how tasteless and sexist). The girl spun around, whipped her arms across her bare chest, ran out of the door, through the snow and into the outhouse.

The deer then turned its brilliant red eyes toward Mary, who was shaking violently in one corner of the small shack. The deer lowered its head like a bull in a ring and slowly moved toward the girl...

A shrill, almost inhuman scream is heard as the movie screen fades to black.

What a movie. I can just see the sequels...

"Bambi's Revenge"

"Blood on Blaze Orange"

and

"Whitetail Terror IV."

Of cupboard creatures creeping

There is at least one horror Stephen King hasn't written about, one terror which has yet to be made into a gross movie for thrill seeking teens.

It is the uppermost shelves of our kitchen cupboards.

Except for the back of the refrigerator and dark recesses of the basement, it is the most feared area of the Oakland household.

I swear, strange things live on those shelves, things born from long forgotten food jars and boxes.

I fully expect one day to find long green tentacles wiggling down from those dark, virtually unexplored shelves. I expect to see thick clinging vines searching for some warm body to wrap around like a boa constrictor and to pull up into the top shelf, there to be devoured ever so slowly by some mutant life form.

Come on, man, you're exaggerating a bit, you say to yourself.

OK, you go after that two-thirds empty bottle of syrup which was last seen on the top shelf during the summer of '83. I dare you.

This colony of creatures has evolved over time.

It began shortly after we moved into our home. Those first

few weeks we filled every cupboard with what we thought were essential provisions.

But a strange thing happened.

Items which were indeed essential in the preparation or enjoyment of food gravitated to the bottom three shelves of the cupboards, those shelves easily reached and easily seen.

Those items which were occasionally used, perhaps once a month, gradually worked their way up to the top shelf. As did those tall bottles and packages which didn't seem to fit on any of the lower shelves.

Over time, bottles and packages placed on the top shelf were pushed back by new bottles and packages. Soon certain items couldn't be seen unless you went up on a stepladder and stood on your tiptoes. And as the saying goes: What isn't seen, isn't remembered.

As the years pass, the contents of these long forgotten groceries oozed out of their containers and mingled with adjacent ooze. Honey joined with a half empty box of macaroni and cheese; popcorn floated on an oil like film of molasses slowly escaping from a cracked bottle. Ant poison used five summers ago merged with a rancid bottle of cooking oil.

Insects found this all a gourmand's delight and flocked to the festering mess. Season after season, generation after generation, these bugs dined on this strange brew. Since no one ever ventured to the top shelf, this biological system went undetected and undisturbed.

That is until the day my wife announced the time had come to clean the cupboards.

"I don't think that's a wise idea," I said as I headed toward the back door.

"Donald! You're not getting out of this. Every time I suggest we clean the cupboards, you disappear. I've never in my life seen a lazier man."

"It's not a question of not wanting to do it, dear. It's just, I'd like to live a little while longer," I pleaded.

"Now, don't start with your cockamamy stories about monsters in the cupboards. I will not have your overactive imagination keeping you from doing a simple, albeit strenuous, household chore," she said angrily.

"OK, OK, " I said as I grabbed a broom.

"What are you doing?"

"Watch."

I lifted the broom toward the top shelf and slowly pushed the bristles into the shadowy recesses of the cupboard. Suddenly the broom shook violently and shot from my hands. For several moments it hung from the top shelf, swaying back and forth like a willow branch. Then, as if thrown by an unseen hand, the broom flew away from the cupboards, shot over my wife's head and struck me on the left side of my face.

I picked it up off the floor. Half the bristles had been eaten away.

Suddenly something within the cupboards made a deep guttural sound, almost like a burp.

We backed away from the cupboards and stared at the dark top shelf. For a moment we thought something with fiery red eyes was staring back at us, but it was only a hint of sunlight reflecting off a bottle of maraschino cherries, left from a cocktail party we suspected occurred during the spring of 1984.

From that day on, we vowed never to trespass upon the top shelf. We figured that so long as we left that community of creatures alone, they would allow us to continue using the bottom three shelves.

Still that day may come when some unsuspecting fellow, a visitor perhaps or relative, will reach for what he or she thinks is a fresh jar of mayonnaise only to be sucked into and absorbed by the shelf that time forgot.

A cure for bat attack

Nothing evokes as much terror in man as the bat.

If one pays a visit to your home, there will be a lot of running and screaming I assure you.

It is truly a brave soul who will go one on one with a flying bat. Dispatching a sleeping bat doesn't count. It's no big deal. It's like hitting a golf ball off a tee.

But a flying bat, now there's a challenge. The darn thing never sits still. It's not like a fly which alights on a window or a lampshade, allowing you to whack it with a rolled up newspaper.

Bats are unique in that they always seem like they're attacking when in actuality they are merely flying by. You see a bat flying within 50 yards of you, you figure he's after your body.

After your hair to be more precise.

I grew up with that myth.

"Bats love to fly into people's hair, particularly long hair. You see a bat, wear a hat," my mother would tell me.

Now if you think about it, why would a bat, or any creature for that matter, want to fly into someone's hair? There's nothing to eat there, and to a bat, our hair must surely smell offensive.

Another reason people don't like bats is the darn things are uglier than sin.

I have to agree.

Next to spiders and rats, bats are the ugliest critters around. Why didn't evolution leave well enough alone when it created mice? Why did it have to go and put wings on them? And why did it make bats fly only at night? Maybe if bats flew in the daytime like songbirds, man would have a better opinion of the creatures.

I feel sorry for bats because there is no way to get rid of them except by killing them.

Ever hear of livetrapping bats? I haven't, except by bat experts who capture them for zoos.

I think it is high time someone designed something better

232

than a tennis racket for dealing with bats.

Can you imagine trying to play tennis with a racket dripping in bat blood?

Why not design a bat vacuum, something on the order of a large ShopVac. You could rent them out like carpet shampooers.

Imagine if you will two scenarios...

Crazy Brooke frantically calls her boyfriend, Stud. She's all upset because there is a bat flying around her bedroom. "Ya gotta come over here right now and kill it, Stud."

A few minutes later, Stud is walking in the front door carrying a $100 graphite tennis racket. "Where is it darling?"

Brooke points to the bedroom. "It'll only be a minute, darlin'" he says confidently.

Suddenly the bat shoots out of the bedroom and right at Stud. He swings the racket blindly, missing the bat completely but hitting squarely a flower vase resting on an end table. Flowers and water explode onto Brooke's new couch.

The bat zooms around the room and makes another pass. Looking somewhat like a hyperactive Jimmy Connors, Stud takes another swing, this time taking the light bulb right out of a ceiling fixture.

Meanwhile, Brooke is running around the room screaming and holding both hands in her hair.

"Shut up Brooke, you're ruining my concentration!" Stud cries out.

Brooke runs into a hall closet and slams the door behind her.

The bat comes in high at 2 o'clock. Stud brings his arm back and then whips the racket as hard as he can. It slams into the poor bat, sending it spinning like a hardball right through the glass door of a china cabinet.

Standing in the dark closet, Brooke only hears the sound of shattering glass and china...and Stud's swearing. She slowly opens the door and looks out. She sees Stud looking at his bent racket with strings looking like someone tore into them with a Mixmaster. Beyond a gaping hole in the china cabinet, a tiny, furry little creature lies dead on a Dwight D. Eisenhower commemorative plate.

Compare that to the following.

Crazy Brooke calls her boyfriend, Ryan. She is frantic because there is a bat flying around her bedroom.

A few minutes later, Ryan appears at the door. He's wearing a navy blue blazer and white pants. "I thought I'd stop by and take care of your bat while on my way to the Country Club."

From a box at his side he pulls out a large cylindrical vacuum cleaner, with a long metal tube attached to a flexible hose.

Suddenly the bat flies out of the bedroom. "Uh, Brooke, before you go into hysterics, do you think you could fetch me an iced tea?"

Brooke runs into the kitchen and slams the door behind her. A minute later, her arm slowly reaches out from the doorway, hands Ryan his glass of tea and quickly retreats behind the closed door.

Ryan takes a sip of his tea while the bat shoots past his head. Then Ryan kicks the vacuum on, takes another swig of tea and points the tube toward the ceiling. Within moments its powerful suction pulls the bat into the vacuum.

"Brooke, you can come out now," Ryan says calmly as he removes from the vacuum a small metal cage and one rather dazed bat. He takes Brooke's hand, walks her to the front door and as he holds her with one arm on her shoulders, he releases the bat. The young couple embrace as they watch the little bat take off to the trees.

You must agree that the second story has a much "batter" ending.

Let's help out the poor maligned bat— someone please develop a bat vacuum.